THE
ABOMINABLE
MAN

THE
ABOMINABLE
MAN

Maj Sjöwall and Per Wahlöö

Translated from the Swedish by Thomas Teal

VINTAGE BOOKS

A Division of Random House, New York

Vintage Books Edition, March 1980

Library of Congress Cataloging in Publication Data
Sjöwall, Maj, 1935—
    The abominable man.
    Translation of Den vedervärdige mannen från Säffle.
    I. Wahlöö, Per, 1926-1975, joint author.   II. Title.
PZ4.S61953Ab 1980   [PT9876.29.J63]   839.7'3'74
ISBN 0-394-74273-7   79-22673

THE
ABOMINABLE
MAN

1.

Just after midnight he stopped thinking.

He'd been writing something earlier, but now the blue ballpoint pen lay in front of him on the newspaper, exactly in the right-hand column of the crossword puzzle. He was sitting erect and utterly motionless on a worn wooden chair in front of a low table in the cramped little attic room. A round yellowish lampshade with a long fringe hung above his head. The fabric was pale with age, and the light from the feeble bulb was hazy and uncertain.

It was quiet in the house. But the quiet was relative —inside there were three people breathing, and from outside came an indistinct, pulsating, barely discernible murmur. As if from traffic on far-off highways, or from a distant boiling sea. The sound of a million human beings. Of a large city in its anxious sleep.

The man in the attic room was dressed in a beige lumberjacket, gray ski pants, a machine-knit black turtleneck sweater and brown ski boots. He had a large but well-tended mustache, just a shade lighter than the hair combed smoothly back at an angle across his head. His face was narrow, with a clean profile and finely chiseled features, and behind the rigid mask of resentful accusation and obstinate purpose there was an almost childlike expression, weak and perplexed and appealing, and nevertheless a little bit calculating.

His clear blue eyes were steady but vacant.

He looked like a little boy grown suddenly very old.

The man sat stock still for almost an hour, the palms of his hands resting on his thighs, his eyes staring blankly at the same spot on the faded flower wallpaper.

Then he stood up, walked across the room, opened a closet door, reached up with his left hand and took something from the shelf. A long thin object wrapped in a white kitchen towel with a red border.

The object was a carbine bayonet.

1

He drew it and very carefully wiped off the yellow gun grease before sliding it into its steel-blue scabbard.

In spite of the fact that he was tall and rather heavy, his movements were quick and lithe and economical, and his hands were as steady as his gaze.

He unbuckled his belt and slid it through the leather loop on the sheath. Then he zipped up his jacket, put on a pair of gloves and a checked tweed cap and left the house.

The wooden stairs creaked beneath his weight, but his footsteps themselves were inaudible.

The house was small and old and stood on the top of a little hill above the highway. It was a chilly, starlit night.

The man in the tweed cap swung around the corner of the house and moved with the sureness of a sleep-walker toward the driveway behind.

He opened the left front door of his black Volkswagen, climbed in behind the wheel and adjusted the bayonet, which rested against his right thigh.

Then he started the motor, turned on the headlights, backed out onto the highway and drove north.

The little black car hurtled forward through the darkness precisely and implacably, as if it were a weightless craft in space.

The buildings tightened along the road and the city rose up beneath its dome of light, huge and cold and desolate, stripped of everything but hard naked surfaces of metal, glass and concrete.

Not even in the central city was there any street life at this hour of the night. With the exception of an occasional taxi, two ambulances and a squad car, everything was dead. The police car was black with white fenders and rushed quickly past on its own bawling carpet of sound.

The traffic lights changed from red to yellow to green to yellow to red with a meaningless mechanical monotony.

The black car drove strictly in accordance with traffic regulations, never exceeded the speed limit, slowed at all cross streets and stopped at all stop lights.

It drove along Vasagatan past the Central Station

and the newly completed Sheraton-Stockholm, swung left at Norra Bantorget and continued north on Torsgatan.

In the square was an illuminated tree and bus 591 waiting at its stop. A new moon hung above St. Eriksplan and the blue neon hands on the Bonnier Building showed the time. Twenty minutes to two.

At that instant, the man in the car was precisely thirty-six years old.

Now he drove east along Odengatan, past deserted Vasa Park with its cold white streetlamps and the thick, veined shadows of ten thousand leafless tree limbs.

The black car made another right and drove one hundred and twenty-five yards south along Dalagatan. Then it braked and stopped.

With studied negligence, the man in the lumberjacket and the tweed cap parked with two wheels on the sidewalk right in front of the stairs to the Eastman Institute.

He stepped out into the night and slammed the door behind him.

It was the third of April, 1971. A Saturday.

It was still only an hour and forty minutes old and nothing in particular had happened.

2.

At a quarter to two the morphine stopped working.

He'd had the last injection just before ten, which meant the narcosis lasted less than four hours.

The pain came back sporadically, first on the left side of his diaphragm and then a few minutes later on the right as well. Then it radiated out toward his back and passed fitfully through his body, quick, cruel and biting, as if starving vultures had torn their way into his vitals.

He lay on his back in the tall, narrow bed and stared at the white plaster ceiling, where the dim glow of the night light and the reflections from outside produced an angular static pattern of shadows that were indecipherable and as cold and repellent as the room itself.

The ceiling wasn't flat but arched in two shallow curves and seemed distant. It was in fact high, over twelve feet, and old-fashioned like everything else in the building. The bed stood in the middle of the stone floor and there were only two other pieces of furniture: the night table and a straight-backed wooden chair.

The drapes were not completely drawn, and the window was ajar. Air filtered chilly and fresh through the two-inch crack from the spring-winter night outside, but he nevertheless felt a suffocating disgust at the rotting odor from the flowers on the night table and from his own sick body.

He had not slept but lain wakeful and silent and thought about this very fact—that the painkiller would soon wear off.

It was about an hour since he'd heard the night nurse pass the double doors to the corridor in her wooden shoes. Since then he'd heard nothing but the sound of his own breathing and maybe of his blood, pulsing heavily and unevenly through his body. But these were not distinct sounds; they were more like figments of his imagination, fitting companions to his dread of the agony that would soon begin and to his mindless fear of dying.

He had always been a hard man, unwilling to tolerate mistakes or weakness in others and never prepared to admit that he himself might someday falter, either physically or mentally.

Now he was afraid and in pain. He felt betrayed and taken by surprise. His senses had sharpened during his weeks in the hospital. He had become unnaturally sensitive to all forms of pain and shuddered even at the prospect of an injection or the needle in the fold of his arm when the nurses took the daily blood tests. On top of that he was afraid of the dark and couldn't stand to be alone and had learned to hear noises he'd never heard before.

The examinations—which ironically enough the doctors referred to as the "investigation"—wore him out and made him feel worse. And the sicker he felt, the more intense his fear of death became, until it circumscribed his entire conscious life and left him utterly naked, in a state of spiritual exposure and almost obscene egoism.

Something rustled outside the window. An animal of course, padding through the withered rose bed. A field mouse or a hedgehog, maybe a cat. But didn't hedgehogs hibernate?

It must be an animal, he thought, and then no longer in control of his actions, he raised his left hand toward the electric call-button that hung in comfortable reach, wound once around the bedpost.

But when his fingers brushed the cold metal of the bed frame, his hand trembled in an involuntary spasm and the switch slid away and fell to the floor with a little rattling bang.

The sound made him pull himself together.

If he'd gotten his hand on the switch and pushed the white button, a red light would have gone on out in the corridor above his door and pretty soon the night nurse would have come trotting from her room in her clattering wooden clogs.

Since he wasn't only afraid but also vain, he was almost glad he hadn't managed to ring.

The night nurse would have come into the room and turned on the overhead light and stared at him questioningly as he lay there in his wretchedness and misery.

He lay still for a while and felt the pain recede and then approach again in sudden waves, as if it were a run-away locomotive driven by an insane engineer.

He suddenly became aware of a new urgency. He needed to urinate.

There was a bottle within reach, stuck down in the yellow plastic wastebasket behind the night table. But he didn't want to use it. He was allowed to get up if he wanted to. One of the doctors had even said it would be good for him to move around a little.

So he thought he'd get up and open the double doors and walk to the toilet, which was right on the other side of the corridor. It was a distraction, a practical task, something that could force his mind into new combinations for a time.

He folded aside the blanket and the sheet, heaved himself into a sitting position and sat for several sec-

onds on the edge of the bed with his feet dangling while
he pulled at the white nightgown and heard the plastic
mattress cover rustling underneath him.

Then he carefully eased himself down until he felt the
cold stone floor beneath the damp soles of his feet. He
tried to straighten up and, in spite of the broad ban-
dages that pulled at his groin and tightened around his
thighs, he succeeded. He was still wearing plastic foam
pressure-dressings from the aortography the day before.

His slippers lay beside the table and he stuck his feet
into them and walked cautiously and gropingly toward
the door. He opened the first door in and the second out
and walked straight across the shadowy corridor and
into the lavatory.

He went to the toilet and rinsed off his hands in cold
water and started back, then stopped in the corridor to
listen. The muffled sound of the night nurse's radio
could be heard a long way off. He was in pain again and
his fear came back and he thought after all he could go
in and ask for a couple of painkillers. They wouldn't
have any particular effect, but anyway she'd have to unlock the medicine cabinet and take out the bottle and
then give him some juice, and that way at least someone
would have to fuss over him for a little while.

The distance to the office was about sixty feet and he
took his time. Shuffled along slowly with the sweaty
nightshirt slapping against his calves.

The light was on in the duty room but there was no
one there. Only the transistor radio, which stood sere-
nading itself between two half-emptied coffee cups.

The night nurse and the orderly were busy someplace
else of course.

The room began to swim and he had to support himself against the door. It felt a little better after a minute
or two, and he walked slowly back toward his room
through the darkened corridor.

The doors were the way he'd left them, slightly ajar.
He closed them carefully, took the few steps to the bed,
stepped out of his slippers, lay down on his back and
pulled the blanket up to his chin with a shiver. Lay still
with wide-open eyes and felt the express train rushing
through his body.

Something was different. The pattern on the ceiling had changed in some slight way.

He was aware of it almost at once.

But what was it that had made the pattern of shadows and reflections change?

His gaze ran over the bare walls, then he turned his head to the right and looked toward the window.

The window had been open when he left the room, he was certain of that.

Now it was closed.

Terror overwhelmed him immediately and he lifted his hand to the call button. But it wasn't in its place. He'd forgotten to pick up the cord and the switch from the floor.

He held his fingers tightly around the iron pipe where the buzzer ought to have been and stared at the window.

The gap between the long drapes was still about two inches wide, but they weren't hanging quite the way they had been, and the window was closed.

Could someone from the staff have been in the room? It didn't seem likely.

He felt the sweat bursting from his pores, and his nightshirt cold and clammy against his sensitive skin.

Completely at the mercy of his fear and unable to tear his eyes from the window, he began to sit up in bed.

The drapes hung absolutely motionless, yet he was certain someone was standing behind them.

Who, he thought.

Who?

And then with a last flash of common sense: This must be a hallucination.

Now he stood beside the bed, ill and unsteady, his bare feet on the stone floor. Took two uncertain steps toward the window. Came to a stop, slightly bent, his lips twitching.

The man in the window alcove threw aside the drapes with his right hand as he simultaneously drew the bayonet with his left.

Reflections glittered on the long broad blade.

The man in the lumberjacket and the checked tweed

cap took two quick steps forward and stopped, legs apart, tall, straight, with the weapon at shoulder height.

The sick man recognized him at once and started to open his mouth to bellow.

The heavy handle of the bayonet hit him across the mouth and he felt his lips being torn to shreds and his dental plate breaking.

And that was the last thing he felt.

The rest of it went too fast. Time rushed away from him.

The first blow caught him on the right side of his diaphragm just below his ribs, and the bayonet sank in to its hilt.

The sick man was still on his feet, his head thrown back, when the man in the lumberjacket raised the weapon for the third time and sliced open his throat, from the left ear to the right.

A bubbling, slightly hissing noise came from the open windpipe.

Nothing more.

3.

It was Friday evening and Stockholm's cafés should have been full of happy people enjoying themselves after the drudgery of the week. Such, however, was not the case, and it wasn't hard to figure out why. In the course of the preceding five years, restaurant prices had as good as doubled, and very few ordinary wage-earners could afford to treat themselves to even one night out a month. The restaurant owners complained and talked crisis, but the ones who had not turned their establishments into pubs or discotheques to attract the easy-spending young managed to keep their heads above water by means of the increasing number of businessmen with credit cards and expense accounts who preferred to conduct their transactions across a laden table.

The Golden Peace in the Old City was no exception. It was late, to be sure—Friday had turned into Saturday

—but during the last hour there had been only two guests in the ground-floor dining room. A man and a woman. They'd eaten steak tartare and were now drinking coffee and *punsch* as they talked in low voices across the table in the alcove.

Two waitresses sat folding napkins at a little table opposite the entrance. The younger, who was red-haired and looked tired, stood up and threw a glance at the clock above the bar. She yawned, picked up a napkin and walked over to the guests in the alcove.

"Will there be anything else before the bar closes?" she said, using the napkin to sweep some crumbs of tobacco from the tablecloth. "Would you care for some more hot coffee, Inspector?"

Martin Beck noticed to his own surprise that he was flattered at her knowing who he was. He was normally irritated by any reminder that as chief of the National Homicide Squad he was a more or less public personage, but it was a long time now since he'd had his picture in the papers or appeared on television, and he took the waitress's recognition only as an indication that the Peace was beginning to regard him as a regular customer. Rightly so, for that matter. He'd been living not far away for two years now, and when he now and again went out to eat he gave his custom mostly to the Peace. Having a companion, as he did this evening, was less usual.

The girl across from him was his daughter, Ingrid. She was nineteen years old, and if you overlooked the fact that she was very blond and he very dark, they were strikingly similar.

"Do you want more coffee?" asked Martin Beck.

Ingrid shook her head and the waitress withdrew to prepare the check. Martin Beck lifted the little bottle of *punsch* from its ice bucket and poured what remained into the two glasses. Ingrid sipped at hers.

"We ought to do this more often," she said.

"Drink *punsch?*"

"Mmm, it is good. No, I mean get together. Next time I'll invite you to dinner. At my place on Klostervägen. You haven't seen it yet."

Ingrid had moved away from home three months before her parents separated. Martin Beck sometimes wondered if he ever would have had the strength to break out of his stagnant marriage to Inga if Ingrid hadn't encouraged him. She hadn't been happy at home and moved in with a friend even before she was out of high school. Now she was studying sociology at the university and had just recently found a one-room apartment in Stocksund. For the time being she was still subletting, but she had prospects of eventually getting the lease on her own.

"Mama and Rolf were out to visit day before yesterday," she said. "I was hoping you'd come too, but I couldn't get hold of you."

"No, I was in Örebro for a couple of days. How are they?"

"Fine. Mama had a whole trunkload of stuff with her. Towels and napkins and that blue coffee service and I don't know what all. Oh, and we talked about Rolf's birthday. Mama wants us to come out and have dinner with them. If you can."

Rolf was three years younger than Ingrid. They were as different as a brother and sister can be, but they'd always gotten along well.

The redhead came with the check. Martin Beck paid and emptied his glass. He looked at his wristwatch. It was a couple of minutes to one.

"Shall we go?" said Ingrid, quickly downing the last few drops of her *punsch*.

They strolled north on Österlånggatan. The stars were out and the air was quite chilly. A couple of drunken teen-agers came walking out of Drakens Gränd, shouting and hollering until the walls of the old buildings echoed with the din.

Ingrid put her hand under her father's arm and suited her stride to his. She was long-legged and slim, almost skinny, Martin Beck thought, but she herself was always saying she'd have to go on a diet.

"Do you want to come up?" he asked on the hill up toward Köpmantorget.

"Yes, but only to call a taxi. It's late, and you have to sleep."

Martin Beck yawned.

"As a matter of fact I am pretty tired," he said.

A man was squatting by the base of the statue of St. George and the Dragon. He seemed to be sleeping, his forehead resting against his knees.

As Ingrid and Martin Beck passed, he lifted his head and said something inarticulate in a high thick voice, then stretched his legs out in front of him and fell asleep again with his chin on his chest.

"Shouldn't he be sleeping it off at Nicolai?" said Ingrid. "It's pretty cold to be sitting outside."

"He'll probably wind up there eventually," Martin Beck said. "If there's room. But it's a long time since it was my job to take care of drunks."

They walked on into Köpmangatan in silence.

Martin Beck was thinking about the summer twenty-two years ago when he'd walked a beat in the Nicolai precinct. Stockholm was a different city then. The Old City had been an idyllic little town. More drunkenness and poverty and misery, of course, before they'd cleared out the slums and restored the buildings and raised the rents so the old tenants could no longer afford to stay. Living here had become fashionable, and he himself was now one of the privileged few.

They rode to the top floor on the elevator, which had been installed when the building was renovated and was one of the few in the Old City. The apartment was completely modernized and consisted of a hall, a small kitchen, a bathroom and two rooms whose windows opened on a large open yard on the east. The rooms were snug and asymmetrical, with deep bay windows and low ceilings. The first of the two rooms was furnished with comfortable easy chairs and low tables and had a fireplace. The inner room contained a broad bed framed by deep built-in shelves and cupboards and, by the window, a huge desk with drawers beneath.

Without taking off her coat, Ingrid went in and sat down at the desk, lifted the receiver and dialed for a taxi.

"Won't you stay for a minute?" Martin called from the kitchen.

"No, I have to go home and get to bed. I'm dead tired. So are you, for that matter."

Martin Beck made no objection. All of a sudden he didn't feel a bit sleepy, but all evening long he'd been yawning, and at the movie—they'd been to see Truffaut's *The 400 Blows*—he'd several times been on the verge of dozing off.

Ingrid finally got hold of a taxi, came out to the kitchen and kissed Martin Beck on the cheek.

"Thanks for a good time. I'll see you at Rolf's birthday if not before. Sleep well."

Martin Beck followed her out to the elevator and whispered good night before closing the doors and going back into his apartment.

He poured the beer he'd taken from the refrigerator into a big glass, walked in and set it on the desk. Then he went to the hi-fi by the fireplace, looked through his records and put one of Bach's Brandenburg Concertos on the turntable. The building was well insulated and he knew he could turn the volume quite high without bothering the neighbors. He sat down at the desk and drank the beer, which was fresh and cold and washed away the sweet sticky taste of *punsch*. He pinched together the paper mouthpiece of a Florida, put the cigarette between his teeth and lit a match. Then he rested his chin in his hands and stared out through the window.

The spring sky arched deep blue and starry above the moonlit roof on the other side of the yard. Martin Beck listened to the music and let his thoughts wander freely. He felt utterly relaxed and content.

When he'd turned the record, he walked over to the shelf above the bed and lifted down a half-completed model of the clipper ship *Flying Cloud*. He worked on masts and yards for almost an hour before putting the model back on its shelf.

While getting undressed, he admired his two completed models with a certain pride—the *Cutty Sark* and the training ship *Danmark*. Soon he'd have only the rigging left to do on the *Flying Cloud*, the most difficult and the most trying part.

He walked naked out to the kitchen and put the ashtray and the beer glass on the counter beside the sink. Then he turned out all the lights except the one above his pillow, closed the bedroom door to a crack and went to bed. He wound the clock, which said two thirty-five, and checked to see that the alarm button was pushed in. He had, he hoped, a free day in front of him and could sleep as long as he liked.

Kurt Bergengren's *Archipelago Steamboats* lay on the night table and he browsed through it, looking at pictures he'd studied carefully before and reading a passage here and a caption there with a strong feeling of nostalgia. The book was large and heavy and not particularly well suited for reading in bed, and his arms were soon tired from holding it. He put it aside and reached out to turn off the reading light.

Then the telephone rang.

4.

Einar Rönn really was dead tired.

He'd been at work for over seventeen hours at a single stretch. Right at the moment, he was standing in the Criminal Division orderly room in the police building of Kungsholmsgatan, looking at a sobbing male adult who had laid hands on one of his fellow men.

For that matter maybe "male adult" was saying too much, since the prisoner was by and large only a child. An eighteen-year-old boy with shoulder-length blond hair, bright red Levi's and a brown suede jacket with a fringe and the word LOVE painted on the back. The letters were surrounded by ornamental flowers in flourishes of pink and violet and baby blue. There were also flowers and words on the legs of his boots, to be exact, the words PEACE and MAGGIE. Long fringes of soft wavy human hair were ingeniously sewn to the jacket's arms.

It was enough to make you wonder if someone hadn't been scalped.

Rönn felt like sobbing himself. Partly from exhaustion, but mostly, as was so often the case these days, because he felt sorrier for the criminal than for the victim.

The young man with the pretty hair had tried to kill a

narcotics pusher. The attempt had not been particularly successful, yet successful enough that the police regarded him as a prime suspect to attempted murder in the second degree.

Rönn had been hunting him since five o'clock that afternoon, which meant he'd been forced to track down and search through no fewer than eighteen narcotics hangouts in different parts of his beautiful city, each one filthier and more repulsive than the one before.

All because some bastard who sold hash mixed with opium to school kids on Mariatorget had gotten a bump on the head. All right, caused by an iron pipe and motivated by the fact that the agent of the blow was broke. But after all, Rönn thought.

Plus: nine hours overtime, which for that matter would be ten before he got home to his apartment in Vällingby.

But you had to take the bad with the good. In this case the good would be the salary.

Rönn was from Lapland, born in Arjeplog and married to a Lappish girl. He didn't particularly like Vällingby, but he liked the name of the street he lived on: Lapland Street.

He looked on while one of his younger colleagues, on night duty, wrote out a receipt for the transfer of the prisoner and delivered up the hair fetish to two guards, who in their turn shoved the prisoner into an elevator for forwarding to the booking section three flights up.

A transfer receipt is a piece of paper bearing the name of the prisoner and binding on no one, on the back of which the duty officer writes appropriate remarks. For example: *Very wild, threw himself again and again against the wall and was injured.* Or: *Uncontrollable, ran into a door and was injured.* Maybe just: *Fell down and hurt himself.*

And so on.

The door from the yard opened and two patrolmen ushered in an older man with a bushy gray beard. Just as they crossed the threshold one of the patrolmen drove his fist into the prisoner's abdomen. The man doubled up and gave out a stifled cry, something like the howl of a dog. The two on-duty detectives shuffled their papers undisturbed.

Rönn threw a tired look at the patrolmen but said nothing.

Then he yawned and looked at his watch.

Seventeen minutes after two.

The telephone rang. One of the detectives answered.

"Yes, this is Criminal, Gustavsson here."

Rönn put on his fur hat and moved toward the door. He had his hand on the knob when the man named Gustavsson stopped him.

"What? Wait a second. Hey, Rönn?"

"Yeah?"

"Here's something for you."

"What now?"

"Something at Mount Sabbath. Somebody's been shot or something. The guy on the phone sounds pretty confused."

Rönn sighed and turned around. Gustavsson took his hand off the receiver.

"One of the boys from Violence is here right now. One of the big wheels. Okay?"

A short pause.

"Yes, yes, I can hear you. It's awful, yes. Now exactly where are you?"

Gustavsson was a thinnish man in his thirties with a tough and impassive air. He listened, then put his hand over the receiver again.

"He's at the main entrance to the central building at Mount Sabbath. Obviously needs help. Are you going?"

"Okay," Rönn said. "I guess I will."

"Do you need a ride? This radio car seems to be free."

Rönn looked a little woefully at the two radio patrolmen and shook his head. They were big and strong and armed with pistols and nightsticks in leather holsters. Their prisoner lay like a whimpering bundle at their feet. They themselves stared jealously and foolishly at Rönn, the hope of promotion in their shallow blue eyes.

"No, I'll take my own car," he said, and left.

Einar Rönn was no big wheel, and right at the moment he didn't feel even like a cog. There were some people who thought he was a very able policeman, and others who said he was typically mediocre. Be that as it might, he had, after years of faithful service, become a deputy inspector on the Violence Squad. A real sleuth, to use the language of the tabloids. That he was peaceable and middle-aged, red-nosed and slightly corpulent from sitting still too much—on those points everyone agreed.

It took him four minutes and twelve seconds to drive to the indicated address.

Mount Sabbath Hospital is spread out over a large, hilly, roughly triangular tract with its base in the north along Vasa Park, its sides along Dalagatan on the east and Torsgatan on the west, and its tip cut off abruptly by the approach to the new bridge over Barnhus Bay. A large brick building belonging to the gas works pushes in from Torsgatan, putting a notch in one corner.

The hospital gets its name from an innkeeper, Vallentin Sabbath, who, at the beginning of the eighteenth century, owned two taverns in the Old City—the Rostock and the Lion. He bought land here and raised carp in ponds that have since dried out or been filled in, and for three years he operated a restaurant on the property before departing this life in 1720.

About ten years later a mineral springs, or spa, was opened on the premises. The two-hundred-year-old mineral springs hotel, which in the course of the years has seen service both as a hospital and a poorhouse, now crouches in the shadow of an eight-story geriatric center.

The original hospital was built a little more than a hundred years ago on the rocky outcropping along Dalagatan and consisted of a number of pavilions connected by long, covered passages. Some of the old pavilions are still in use, but a number of them have quite recently been torn down and replaced by new ones, and the system of passages is now underground.

At the far end of the grounds stand a number of older buildings that house the old people's home. There is a little chapel here, and in the middle of a garden of lawns and hedges and gravel walks there is a yellow summerhouse with white trim and a spire on its rounded roof. An avenue of trees leads from the chapel to an old gatehouse down by the street. Behind the chapel the grounds rise higher only to come to a sudden stop above Torsgatan, which curves between the cliff and the Bonnier Building across the way. This is the quietest and least frequented part of the hospital area. The main entrance is on Dalagatan where it was a hundred years ago, and next to it is the new central hospital building.

5.

Rönn felt almost ghostlike in the blue light flashing from the roof of the patrol car. But it would soon get worse.

"What's happened?" he said.

"Don't know for sure. Something ugly."

The patrolman looked very young. His face was open and sympathetic, but his glance wandered and he seemed to be having trouble standing still. He was holding onto the car door with his left hand and fingering the butt of his pistol a little hesitantly with his right. Ten seconds earlier he'd made a sound that could only have been a sigh of relief.

The boy's scared, Rönn thought. He made his voice reassuring.

"Well, we'll see. Where is it?"

"It's kind of hard to get there. I'll drive in front."

Rönn nodded and went back to his own car. Started the motor and followed the blue flashes in a wide swing around the central hospital and into the grounds. In the course of thirty seconds the patrol car made three right turns, two left turns, then braked and stopped outside a long low building with yellow plaster walls and a black mansard roof. It looked ancient. Above the weathered wooden door a single flickering bulb in an old-fashioned milkglass globe was fighting what was pretty much a losing battle against the darkness. The patrolman climbed out and assumed his former stance, fingers on car door and pistol butt as a kind of shield against the night and what it might be presumed to conceal.

"In there," he said, glancing guardedly at the double wooden door.

Rönn stifled a yawn and nodded.

"Shall I call for more men?"

"Well, we'll see," Rönn repeated good-naturedly.

He was already on the steps pushing open the right-hand half of the door, which creaked mournfully on un-oiled hinges. Another couple of steps and another door and he found himself in a sparsely lit corridor. It was broad and high-ceilinged and stretched the entire length of the building.

On one side were private rooms and wards, the other was apparently reserved for lavatories and linen closets and examination rooms. On the wall was an old black pay phone of the kind that only cost ten öre to use. Rönn stared at an oval white enamel plate with the laconic inscription ENEMA and then went on to study the four people he could see from where he stood.

Two of them were uniformed policemen. One of these was stocky and solid and stood with feet apart and his arms at his sides and his eyes straight ahead. In his left hand he was holding an open notebook with black covers. His colleague was leaning against the wall, head down, his gaze directed into an enameled cast-iron washbasin with an old-fashioned brass spigot. Of all the young men Rönn had encountered during his nine hours of overtime, this one looked to be easily the youngest. In his leather jacket and shoulder belt and apparently indispensable weaponry, he looked like a paro-dy of a policeman. An older gray-haired woman with glasses sat collapsed in a wicker chair, staring apatheti-cally at her white wooden clogs. She was wearing a white smock and had an ugly case of varicose veins on her pale calves. The quartet was completed by a man in his thirties. He had curly black hair and was biting his knuckles in irritation. He too was wearing a white coat and wood-soled shoes.

The air in the corridor was unpleasant and smelled of disinfectant, vomit, or medicine, or maybe all three at once. Rönn sneezed suddenly and unexpectedly and, a little late, grabbed his nose between thumb and forefinger.

The only one to react was the policeman with the notebook. Without saying anything, he pointed to a tall door with light yellow crackled paint and a typewritten white card in a metal frame. The door was not quite closed. Rönn plucked it open without touching the handle. Inside there was another door. That one too was ajar, but opened in.

Rönn pushed it with his foot, looked into the room and gave a start. He let go of his reddish nose and took another look, this one more systematic.

"My, my," he said to himself.

Then he took a step backward, let the outer door swing back to its former position, put on his glasses and examined the nameplate.

"Jesus," he said.

The policeman had put away the black notebook and had taken out his badge instead, which he now stood fingering as if it had been a rosary or an amulet.

Police badges were soon to be eliminated, Rönn remembered, irrationally. And with that, the long battle as to whether badges should be worn on the chest as forthright identification or hidden away in a pocket somewhere had come to a disappointing as well as surprising conclusion. They were simply done away with, replaced by ordinary ID cards, and policemen could safely go on hiding behind the anonymity of the uniform.

"What's your name?" he said out loud.

"Andersson."

"What time did you get here?"

The policeman looked at his wristwatch.

"At two sixteen. Nine minutes ago. We were right in the neighborhood. At Odenplan."

Rönn took off his glasses and glanced at the uniformed boy, who was light green in the face and vomiting helplessly into the sink. The older patrolman followed his look.

"He's just a cadet," he said under his breath. "It's his first time out."

"Better give him a hand," said Rönn. "And send out a call for five or six men from the Fifth."

"The emergency bus from Precinct Five, yes sir," Andersson said, looking as if he were about to salute or snap to attention or some other dumb thing.

"Just a moment," Rönn said. "Have you seen anything suspicious around here?"

He hadn't put it so awfully well perhaps, and the patrolman stared bewilderedly at the door to the sickroom.

"Well, ah . . ." he said evasively.

"Do you know who that is? The man in there?"

"Chief Inspector Nyman, isn't it?"

"Yes, it is."

"Though you can't hardly tell by looking."

"No," Rönn said. "Not hardly."

Andersson went out.

Rönn wiped the sweat from his forehead and considered what he ought to do.

For ten seconds. Then he walked over to the pay phone and dialed Martin Beck's home number.

"Hi. It's Rönn. I'm at Mount Sabbath. Come on over."

"Okay," said Martin Beck.

"Quick."

"Okay."

Rönn hung up the receiver and went back to the others. Waited. Gave his handkerchief to the cadet, who self-consciously wiped off his mouth.

"I'm sorry," he said.

"It can happen to anyone."

"I couldn't help it. Is it always like this?"

"No," Rönn said. "I wouldn't say that. I've been a policeman for twenty-one years and to be honest I've never seen anything like this before."

Then he turned to the man with the curly black hair.

"Is there a psychiatric ward here?"

"*Nix verstehen,*" the doctor said.

Rönn put on his glasses and examined the plastic name badge on the doctor's white coat.

Sure enough, there was his name.

DR. ÜZK ÜKÖCÖTÜPZE.

"Oh," he said to himself.

Put away his glasses and waited.

6.

The room was fifteen feet long, ten feet wide, and almost twelve feet high. The colors were very drab—ceiling a dirty white and the plastered walls an indefinite grayish yellow. Gray-white marble tiles on the floor. Light gray window-frames and door. In front of the window hung heavy pale-yellow damask drapes and, behind them, thin white cotton curtains. The iron bed was white, likewise the sheets and pillowcase. The night table was gray and the wooden chair light brown. The paint on the furniture was worn, and on the rough walls it was crackled with age. The plaster on the ceiling was flaking and in several places there were light brown spots where moisture had seeped through. Everything was old but very clean. On the table was a nickel silver vase with seven pale red roses. Plus a pair of glasses and a glasses case, a transparent plastic beaker containing two small white tablets, a little white transistor radio, a half-eaten apple, and a tumbler half full of some bright yellow liquid. On the shelf below lay a pile of magazines, four letters, a tablet of lined paper, a shiny Waterman pen with ballpoint cartridges in four different colors, and some loose change—to be exact, eight ten-öre pieces, two twenty-five-öre pieces, and six one-crown coins. The table had two drawers. In the upper one were three used handkerchiefs, a bar of soap in a plastic box, toothpaste, toothbrush, a small bottle of after-shave, a box of cough drops, and a leather case with a nail clipper, file and scissors. The other contained a wallet, an electric razor, a small folder of postage stamps, two pipes, a tobacco pouch and a blank picture postcard of the Stockholm city hall. There were some clothes hanging over the back of the straight chair —a gray cotton coat, pants of the same color and material, and a knee-length white shirt. Underwear and socks lay on the seat, and next to the bed stood a pair of slippers. A beige bathrobe hung on the clothes hook by the door.

There was only one completely dissident color in the room. And that was a shocking red.

The dead man lay partly on his side between the bed and the window. The throat had been cut with such force that the head had been thrown back at an angle of almost ninety degrees and lay with its left cheek against the floor. The tongue had forced its way out through the gaping incision and the victim's broken false teeth stuck out between the mutilated lips.

As he fell backward a thick stream of blood had pumped out through the carotid artery. This explained the crimson streak across the bed and the splashes of blood on the flower vase and night table.

On the other hand it was the wound in the midriff that had soaked the victim's shirt and provided the enormous pool of blood around the body. A superficial inspection of this wound indicated that someone, with a single blow, had cut through the liver, bile ducts, stomach, spleen and pancreas. Not to mention the aorta.

Virtually all the blood in the body had welled out in the course of a few seconds. The skin was bluish white and seemed almost transparent, where, that is, it could be seen at all, for example on the forehead and parts of the shins and feet.

The lesion on the torso was about ten inches long and wide open; the lacerated organs had pressed out between the sliced edges of the peritoneum.

The man had virtually been cut in two.

Even for people whose job it was to linger at the scenes of macabre and bloody crimes, this was strong stuff.

But Martin Beck's expression hadn't changed since he entered the room. To an outside observer it would have seemed almost as if everything were part of the routine—going to the Peace with his daughter, eating, drinking, getting undressed, pottering with a ship model, going to bed with a book. And then suddenly rushing off to inspect a slaughtered chief inspector of police. The worst part was that he felt that way himself.

He never allowed himself to be taken aback, except by his own emotional coolness.

It was now three ten in the morning and he sat on his haunches beside the bed and surveyed the body, coldly and appraisingly.

"Yes, it's Nyman," he said.

"Yes, I guess it is."

Rönn stood poking among the objects on the table. All at once he yawned and put his hand guiltily to his mouth.

Martin Beck threw him a quick glance.

"Have you got some sort of timetable?"

"Yes," Rönn said.

He pulled out a small notebook where he'd made some industrious jotting in a tiny, stingy hand. Put on his glasses and rattled it off in a monotone.

"An assistant nurse opened those doors at ten minutes after two. Hadn't heard or seen anything unusual. Making a routine check on the patients. Nyman was dead then. She dialed 90-000 at two eleven. The patrolmen in the radio car got the alarm at two twelve. They were at Odenplan and made it here in between three and four minutes. They reported to Criminal at two seventeen. I got here at two twenty-two. Called you at two twenty-nine. You got here at sixteen minutes to three."

Rönn looked at his watch.

"It's now eight minutes to three. When I arrived he'd been dead at the most half an hour."

"Is that what the doctor said?"

"No, that's my own conclusion, so to speak. The warmth of the body, coagulation——"

He stopped, as if it had been presumptuous to mention his own observations.

Martin Beck rubbed the bridge of his nose thoughtfully with the thumb and forefinger of his right hand.

"So then everything happened very fast," he said.

Rönn didn't answer. He seemed to be thinking about something else.

"Well," he said after a while, "you understand why it was I called you. Not because——"

He stopped, seeming somehow distracted.

"Not because?"

"Not because Nyman was a chief inspector, but because . . . well, because of this."

Rönn gestured vaguely toward the body.

"He was butchered."

He paused for a second and then came up with a new conclusion.

"I mean, whoever did this must be raving mad."

Martin Beck nodded.

"Yes," he said. "It looks that way."

7.

Martin Beck was beginning to feel ill at ease. The sensation was vague and hard to trace, somewhat like the sneaking fatigue when you're falling asleep over a book and go on reading without turning any pages.

He'd have to make an effort to gather his wits and get a grip on these slippery apprehensions.

Closely related to this lurking sensation of impotence, there was another feeling he couldn't seem to get rid of.

A sense of danger.

That something was about to happen. Something that had to be warded off at any price. But he didn't know what, and still less how.

He'd had such feelings before, if only at long intervals. His colleagues tended to laugh off this phenomenon and call it intuition.

Police work is built on realism, routine, stubbornness and system. It's true that a lot of difficult cases are cleared up by coincidence, but it's equally true that coincidence is an elastic concept that mustn't be confused with luck or accident. In a criminal investigation, it's a question of weaving the net of coincidence as fine as possible. And experience and industry play a larger role there than brilliant inspiration. A good memory and ordinary common sense are more valuable qualities than intellectual brilliance.

Intuition has no place in practical police work.

Intuition is not even a quality, any more than astrology and phrenology are sciences.

And still it was there, however reluctant he was to admit it, and there had been times when it seemed to have put him on the right track.

And yet his ambivalence might also depend on simpler, more tangible and immediate things.

On Rönn, for example.

Martin Beck expected a great deal of the people he worked with. The blame for that fell on Lennart Kollberg, for many years his right-hand man, first when he was a city detective in Stockholm and then later at the old National Criminal Division in Västberga. Kollberg had always been his surest complement, the man who played the best shots, asked the right leading questions and gave the proper cues.

But Kollberg wasn't available. He was at home asleep, presumably, and there was no acceptable reason for waking him. It would be against the rules, and an insult to Rönn what's more.

Martin Beck expected Rönn to do something or at least say something that showed he too sensed the danger. That he would come up with some assertion or supposition that Martin Beck could refute or pursue.

But Rönn said nothing.

Instead he did his job calmly and capably. The investigation was for the moment his, and he was doing everything that could reasonably be expected.

The area outside the window had been cordoned off with ropes and sawhorses, patrol cars had been driven up and headlights lit. Spotlights swept the terrain and small white patches of light from police flashlights wandered jerkily across the ground like frightened sand crabs across a beach in unorganized flight from approaching intruders.

Rönn had gone through what there was on and in the night table without finding anything but ordinary personal belongings and a few trivial letters of the insensitively hearty type that healthy people write to individuals who are suspected of being seriously ill. Civilian personnel from the Fifth Precinct had gone through the adjoining rooms and wards without finding anything of note.

If Martin Beck wanted to know anything in particular, he would have to ask, and furthermore would have to formulate his question clearly, in phrases that could not be misunderstood.

The truth of the matter was simply that they worked together badly. Both of them had discovered this years before, and they therefore generally avoided situations where they had only one another to fall back on.

Martin Beck's opinion of Rönn was none too high, a circumstance the latter was well aware of and which gave him an inferiority complex. Martin Beck, for his part, recognized as his own failing a difficulty in establishing contact and thus became inhibited himself.

Rönn had produced the beloved old murder kit, secured a number of fingerprints, and had plastic covers placed over several pieces of evidence in the room and on the ground outside, thereby ensuring that details that might prove valuable later on would not be effaced by natural causes or destroyed by carelessness. These pieces of evidence were mostly footprints.

Martin Beck had a cold, as usual at this time of year. He snuffled and blew his nose and coughed and hacked and Rönn didn't react. He did not, as a matter of fact, even say "Bless you." This small civility was apparently not a part of his upbringing, nor of his vocabulary. And if he thought anything, he kept it to himself.

There was no tacit communication between them and Martin Beck felt himself called upon to break the silence.

"Doesn't this whole ward seem a little old-fashioned?" he asked.

"Yes," Rönn said. "It's supposed to be vacated the day after tomorrow and modernized or turned into something else. The patients are going to be moved to new wards in the central building."

Martin Beck's thoughts moved promptly off in new directions.

"I wonder what he used," he said a while later, mostly to himself. "Maybe a machete or a samurai sword."

"Neither one," said Rönn, who had just come into

the room. "We've found the weapon. It's lying outside, about twelve feet from the window."

They went outside and looked.

In the cold white light of a spot lay a broad-bladed cutting tool.

"A bayonet," said Martin Beck.

"Yes. Exactly. For a Mauser carbine."

The six-millimeter carbine had been a common military weapon, used mostly by the artillery and cavalry. Martin Beck had one himself when he did his national service. The weapon had probably gone out of use by now and been stricken from the quartermaster's rolls.

The blade was entirely covered with clotted blood.

"Can you get fingerprints from that grooved handle?"

Rönn shrugged his shoulders.

Every word had to be dragged from him, if not by force then anyway by verbal pressure.

"You're letting it lie there until it gets light?"

"Yes," Rönn said. "Seems like a good idea."

"I'd very much like to talk to Nyman's family as soon as possible. Do you think we could get his wife out of bed at this hour?"

"Yes, I guess so," said Rönn without conviction.

"We have to start someplace. Are you coming along?"

Rönn mumbled something.

"What'd you say?" said Martin Beck and blew his nose.

"Got to get a photographer out here," Rönn said. "Yeah."

But he didn't sound at all as if he cared.

8.

Rönn walked out to the car and got into the driver's seat to wait for Martin Beck, who'd taken upon himself the unpleasant task of calling the widow.

"How much did you tell her?" he asked when Martin Beck had climbed in beside him.

"Only that he's dead. He was apparently seriously ill, so maybe it didn't come as such a surprise. But of course now she's wondering what we've got to do with it."

"How did she sound? Shocked?"

"Yes, of course. She was going to jump in a taxi and come straight over to the hospital. There's a doctor talking to her now. I hope he manages to convince her to wait at home."

"Yes. If she saw him now she'd really get a shock. It's bad enough having to tell her about it."

Rönn drove north on Dalagatan toward Odengatan. Outside the Eastman Institute stood a black Volkswagen. Rönn nodded toward it.

"Not bad enough he parks in a no-parking zone, he's halfway up on the sidewalk too. Lucky for him we're not from Traffic."

"On top of which he must have been drunk to park like that," said Martin Beck.

"Or she," Rönn said. "It must be a woman. Women and cars . . ."

"Typical stereotyped thinking," said Martin Beck. "If my daughter could hear you now you'd get a real lecture."

The car swung right on Odengatan and drove on past Gustav Vasa Church and Odenplan. At the taxi station there were two cabs with their FREE signs lit, and at the traffic signal outside the city library there was a yellow street-cleaning machine with a blinking orange light on its roof, waiting for the light to turn green.

Martin Beck and Rönn drove on in silence. They turned on to Sveavägen and passed the street-sweeper as it rumbled around the corner. At the School of Economics they took a left on to Kungstensgatan.

"Damn it to hell," said Martin Beck suddenly with emphasis.

"Yeah," said Rönn.

Then it was quiet again in the car. When they'd crossed Birger Jarlsgatan, Rönn slowed down and started hunting for the number. An apartment house door opened across from the Citizens School and a young man stuck out his head and looked in their direction.

He held the door open while they parked the car and crossed the street.

When they reached the doorway they saw that the boy was younger than he'd looked from a distance. He was almost as tall as Martin Beck, but looked to be fifteen years old at the most.

"My name's Stefan," he said. "Mother's waiting upstairs."

They followed him up the stairs to the second floor, where a door stood ajar. The boy showed them through the front hall and into the living room.

"I'll get Mother," he mumbled and disappeared into the hall.

Martin Beck and Rönn remained standing in the middle of the room and looked around. It was very neat. One side was taken up by a suite of furniture that seemed to date from the 1940's and consisted of a sofa, three matching easy chairs in varnished blond wood and flowered cretonne upholstery, and an oval table of the same light wood. A white lace cloth lay on the table, and in the middle of the cloth was a large crystal vase of red tulips. The two windows looked out on the street, and behind the white lace curtains stood rows of well-tended potted plants. The wall at one end of the room was covered by a bookcase in gleaming mahogany, half filled with leather-bound books, half with souvenirs and small knickknacks. Small polished tables with pieces of silver and crystal stood here and there against the walls. A black piano with the lid closed over the keyboard completed the list of furniture. Framed portraits of the family stood lined up on the piano. Several still lifes and landscapes in wide ornate gold frames hung on the walls. A crystal chandelier burned in the middle of the room, and a wine-red Oriental rug lay beneath their feet.

Martin Beck took in the various details of the room as he listened to the footsteps approaching in the hall. Rönn had walked up to the bookcase and was suspiciously eying a brass reindeer-bell, one side of which was adorned with a brightly colored picture of a mountain birch, a reindeer and a Lapp, plus the word ARJEPLOG in ornate red letters.

Mrs. Nyman came into the room with her son. She was wearing a black wool dress, black shoes and stockings, and held a small white handkerchief clenched in one hand. She had been crying.

Martin Beck and Rönn introduced themselves. She didn't look as if she'd ever heard of them.

"But please sit down," she said, and took a seat in one of the flowered chairs.

When the two policemen had seated themselves she looked at them with despair in her eyes.

"What is it that's happened actually?" she asked in a voice that was much too shrill.

Rönn took out his handkerchief and began to polish his florid nose, thoroughly and at length. But Martin Beck hadn't expected any help from that quarter.

"If you have anything to calm your nerves, Mrs. Nyman—pills I mean—I think it would be wise to take a couple now," he said.

The boy, who had taken a seat on the piano stool, stood up.

"Papa has . . . There's a bottle of Restenil in the cabinet in the bathroom," he said. "Shall I get it?"

Martin Beck nodded and the boy went out to the bathroom and came back with the tablets and a glass of water. Martin Beck looked at the label, shook out two tablets into the lid of the bottle and handed them to Mrs. Nyman, who obediently swallowed them with a gulp of water.

"Thank you," she said. "Now please tell me what it is you want. Stig is dead, and neither you nor I can do anything about that."

She pressed the handkerchief to her mouth, and her voice was stifled when she spoke.

"Why wasn't I allowed to go to him? He's my husband after all. What have they done to him there at the hospital? That doctor . . . he sounded so odd . . ."

Her son went over and sat on the arm of her chair. He put his arm around her shoulders.

Martin Beck twisted in his chair so that he sat directly facing her, then he threw a glance at Rönn, sitting silently on the sofa.

"Mrs. Nyman," he said, "your husband did not die of his illness. Someone entered his room and killed him."

The woman stared at him and he could see in her eyes that several seconds passed before she understood the significance of what he'd said. She lowered the hand with the handkerchief and pressed it to her breast. She was very pale.

"Killed? Someone killed him? I don't understand . . ."

The son had gone white around the nostrils and his grip around his mother's shoulders tightened.

"Who?" he said.

"We don't know. A nurse found him on the floor of his room just after two o'clock. Someone had come in through the window and killed him with a bayonet. It must have happened in the course of a few seconds, I don't think he had time to realize what was happening."

Said Martin Beck. The giver of comfort.

"Everything indicates he was taken by surprise," Rönn said. "If he'd had time to react he would have tried to protect himself or ward off the blows, but there's no sign that he did."

The woman now stared at Rönn.

"But why?" she said.

"We don't know," Rönn said.

That was all he said.

"Mrs. Nyman, maybe you can help us find out," said Martin Beck. "We don't want to cause you unnecessary pain, but we have to ask you a few questions. First of all, can you think of anyone who might have done it?"

The woman shook her head hopelessly.

"Do you know if your husband had ever received any threats? Or if there was anyone who thought he had reason to want to see him dead? Anyone who threatened him?"

She went on shaking her head.

"No," she said. "Why should anyone threaten him?"

"Anyone who hated him?"

"Why should anyone hate him?"

"Think carefully," Martin Beck said. "Wasn't there anyone who thought your husband had treated him badly? He was a policeman after all, and making ene-

mies is part of the job. Did he ever say someone was out
to get him or had threatened him?"

The widow looked in confusion first at her son, then
at Rönn, and then back at Martin Beck.

"Not that I can recall. And I'd certainly remember if
he'd said anything like that."

"Papa didn't talk much about his job," Stefan said.
"You'd better ask at the station."

"We'll ask there too," said Martin Beck. "How long
had he been sick?"

"A long time, I don't remember exactly," the boy
said, and looked at his mother.

"Since June of last year," she said. "He got sick just
before Midsummer, an awful pain in his stomach, and
he went to the doctor right after the holiday. The doctor
thought it was an ulcer and had him go on sick leave.
He's been on sick leave ever since, and he's been to several different doctors and they all say different things
and prescribe different medicines. Then three weeks
ago he went into Sabbath and they've been examining
him and doing a lot of tests ever since, but they
couldn't find out what it was."

Talking seemed to distract her attention and help her
repress the shock.

"Papa thought it was cancer," the boy said. "But the
doctors said it wasn't. But he was awful sick all the
time."

"What did he do all this time? Hasn't he worked at
all since last summer?"

"No," Mrs. Nyman said. "He was really very ill. Had
attacks of pain that lasted several days in a row when
all he could do was lie in bed. He took a lot of pills, but
they didn't help much. He went down to the station a
few times last fall to see how things were going, as he
said, but he couldn't work."

"And Mrs. Nyman, you can't remember anything he
said or did that might have some connection with what's
happened?" asked Martin Beck.

She shook her head and started sobbing dryly. Her
eyes glided on past Martin Beck and she stared straight
ahead at nothing.

"Do you have any brothers and sisters?" Rönn asked the boy.

"Yes, a sister, but she's married and lives in Malmö."

Rönn glanced inquiringly at Martin Beck, who was rolling a cigarette thoughtfully back and forth between his fingers as he looked at the two people in front of him.

"We'll be going now," he said to the boy. "I'm sure you can take care of your mother, but I think the best thing would be if you could get a doctor to come over and give her something to make her sleep. Is there any doctor you can call at this time of night?"

The boy stood up and nodded.

"Doctor Blomberg," he said. "He usually comes when someone in the family's sick."

He went out in the hall and they heard him dial a number and after a while someone seemed to answer. The conversation was short and he came back and stood beside his mother. He looked more like an adult now than he had when they first saw him down in the doorway.

"He's coming," the boy said. "You don't need to wait. It won't take him long."

They stood up and Rönn went over and put his hand on the woman's shoulder. She didn't move, and when they said good-bye she didn't respond.

The boy went with them to the door.

"We may have to come back," said Martin Beck. "We'll call you first to find out how your mother's doing."

When they were out on the street he turned to Rönn.

"I suppose you knew Nyman?" he said.

"Not especially well," said Rönn evasively.

9.

The blue-white light of a flashbulb lit the dirty yellow façade of the hospital pavilion for an instant as Martin Beck and Rönn returned to the scene of the crime. An additional couple of cars had arrived and stood parked in the turnaround with their headlights on.

"Apparently our photographer is here," Rönn said.

The photographer came toward them as they got out of the car. He carried no camera bag but held his camera and flash in one hand, while his pockets bulged with rolls of film and flashbulbs and lenses. Martin Beck recognized him from the scenes of previous crimes.

"Wrong," he said to Rönn. "It looks like the papers got here first."

The photographer, who worked for one of the tabloids, greeted them and took a picture as they walked toward the door. A reporter from the same paper was standing at the foot of the stairs trying to talk to a patrolman.

"Good morning, Inspector," he said when he caught sight of Martin Beck. "I don't suppose I could follow you in?"

Martin Beck shook his head and walked up the steps with Rönn in his wake.

"But you'll give me a little interview at least?" the reporter said.

"Later," said Martin Beck and held the door open for Rönn before closing it right on the nose of the reporter, who made a face.

The police photographer had also arrived and was standing outside the dead man's room with his camera bag. Farther down the corridor was the doctor with the curious name and a plainclothes detective from the Fifth. Rönn went into the sickroom with the photographer and put him to work. Martin Beck walked over to the two men in the hall.

"How's it going?" he said.

34

The same old question.

The plainclothesman, whose name was Hansson, scratched the back of his neck.

"We've talked to most of the patients in this corridor, and none of them saw or heard anything. I was just trying to ask Doctor . . . uh . . . this doctor here, when we can talk to the other ones."

"Have you questioned the people in the adjoining rooms?" Martin Beck asked.

"Yes," Hansson said. "And we've been in all the wards. No one heard anything, but then the walls are thick in a building this old."

"We can wait with the others till breakfast," said Martin Beck.

The doctor said nothing. He obviously didn't understand Swedish, and after a while he pointed toward the office and said, "Have to go," in English.

Hansson nodded, and the black curls hurried off in clattering wooden shoes.

"Did you know Nyman?" asked Martin Beck.

"Well, no, not really. I've never worked in his precinct, but of course we've met often enough. He's been around a long time. He was already an inspector when I started, twelve years ago."

"Do you know anyone who knew him well?"

"You can always ask down at Klara," Hansson said. "That's where he was before he got sick."

Martin Beck nodded and looked at the electric wall clock over the door to the washroom. It said a quarter to five.

"I guess I'll go on over there for a while," he said. "There's not much I can do here for the moment."

"Go on," said Hansson. "I'll tell Rönn where you went."

Martin Beck took a deep breath when he got outside. The chilly night air felt fresh and clean. The reporter and the photographer were nowhere to be seen, but the patrolman was still standing at the foot of the steps.

Martin Beck nodded to him and started walking toward the parking lot.

The center of Stockholm had been subjected to
sweeping and violent changes in the course of the last
ten years. Entire districts had been leveled and new
ones constructed. The structure of the city had been altered: streets had been broadened and freeways built.
What was behind all this activity was hardly an ambi-
tion to create a humane social environment but rather a
desire to achieve the fullest possible exploitation of
valuable land. In the heart of the city it had not been
enough to tear down ninety percent of the buildings and
completely obliterate the original street plan, violence
had been visited on the natural topography itself.

Stockholm's inhabitants looked on with sorrow and
bitterness as serviceable and irreplaceable old apartment houses were razed to make way for sterile office
buildings. Powerless, they let themselves be deported to
distant suburbs while the pleasant, lively neighborhoods
where they had lived and worked were reduced to rub-
ble. The inner city became a clamorous, all but impass-
able construction site from which the new city slowly
and relentlessly arose with its broad, noisy traffic arter-
ies, its shining façades of glass and light metal, its dead
surfaces of flat concrete, its bleakness and its desola-
tion.

In this frenzy of modernization, the city's police sta-
tions seemed to have been completely overlooked. All
the station houses in the inner city were old-fashioned
and the worse for wear, and in most cases, since the
force had been enlarged over the years, crowded. In the
Fourth Precinct, where Martin Beck was on his way,
this lack of space was one of the primary problems.

By the time he stepped out of the taxi in front of the
Klara police station on Regeringsgatan, it had begun to
get light. The sun would come up, there was still not a
cloud in the sky, and it promised to be a pretty though
rather chilly day.

He walked up the stone steps and pushed open the
door. To the right was the switchboard, for the moment
unmanned, and a counter behind which stood an older,
gray-haired policeman. He had spread out the morning

paper and was resting on his elbows as he read. When Martin Beck came in he straightened up and took off his glasses.

"Why it's Inspector Beck, up and about at this time of the morning," he said. "I was just looking to see if the morning papers had anything about Inspector Nyman. It sounds like a very nasty business."

He put on his glasses again, licked his thumb and turned a page in the paper.

"It doesn't look like they had time to get it in," he went on.

"No," said Martin Beck. "I don't suppose they did."

The Stockholm morning papers went to press early these days and had probably been ready for distribution even before Nyman was murdered.

He walked past the desk and into the duty room. It was empty. The morning papers lay on a table along with a couple of overflowing ashtrays and some coffee mugs. Through a window into one of the interrogation rooms he could see the officer in charge sitting talking to a young woman with long blond hair. When he caught sight of Martin Beck he stood up, said something to the woman and came out of the glass cubicle. He closed the door behind him.

"Hi," he said. "Is it me you're looking for?"

Martin Beck sat down at the short end of the table, pulled an ashtray toward him and lit a cigarette.

"I'm not looking for anyone in particular," he said. "But have you got a minute?"

"Can you wait just a moment?" the other man said. "I just want to get this woman sent over to Criminal."

He disappeared and returned a few minutes later with a radio patrolman, picked up an envelope from the desk and handed it to him. The woman stood up, hung her purse on her shoulder and walked quickly toward the door.

"Come on, big boy," she said without turning her head. "Let's go for a ride."

The patrolman looked at the officer, who shrugged his shoulders, amused. Then he put on his cap and followed her out.

"She seemed right at home," said Martin Beck.

"Oh yeah, this isn't the first time. And certainly not the last."

He sat down at the table and started cleaning his pipe into an ashtray.

"That was nasty, that business with Nyman," he said. "How did it happen, actually?"

Martin Beck told him briefly what had happened.

"Ugh," the officer said. "Whoever did it must be a raving lunatic. But why Nyman?"

"You knew Nyman, didn't you?" Martin Beck asked him.

"Not very well. He wasn't the sort of person you knew well."

"He was here on special assignment of course. When did he come here to the Fourth?"

"They gave him an office here three years ago. February '68."

"What sort of a person was he?" Martin Beck asked.

The officer filled his pipe and lit it before answering.

"I don't really know how to describe him. You knew him too, I suppose? Ambitious you could certainly call him, stubborn, not much of a sense of humor. Pretty conservative in his views. The younger fellows were a little afraid of him, in spite of the fact they didn't really have anything to do with him. He could be pretty stern. But like I said, I didn't know him at all well."

"Did he have any particular friends on the force?"

"Not here anyway. I don't think he and our inspector got along very well. But otherwise I don't know."

The man thought for a moment and then looked at Martin Beck oddly—appealingly and conspiratorially.

"Well . . ." he said.

"What?"

"I mean I guess he still had friends at headquarters, didn't he?"

Martin Beck didn't answer. Instead he put another question.

"What about enemies?"

"Don't know. He probably had enemies, but hardly here, and certainly not to the point that . . ."

"Do you know if he'd been threatened?"

"No, he didn't exactly confide in me. Although for that matter . . ."

"Yes, what?"

"Well, for that matter, Nyman wasn't the kind of man who let himself be threatened."

The telephone rang inside the glass cubicle and the officer went in and answered it. Martin Beck walked over and stood by the window with his hands in his pockets. The station house was quiet. The only sounds to be heard were the voice of the man on the telephone and the dry coughing of the old policeman at the switchboard. Presumably things were not so quiet in the arrest section on the floor below.

Martin Beck suddenly realized how tired he was. His eyes ached from lack of sleep, and his throat from way too many cigarettes.

The phone call looked like it was going to be a long one. Martin Beck yawned and leafed through the morning paper, read the headlines and an occasional picture caption but without really seeing what he read. Finally he folded up the paper, walked over and knocked on the window to the cubicle, and when the man on the phone looked up he made signs indicating he was about to leave. The officer waved and went on talking into the receiver.

Martin Beck lit another cigarette and thought distractedly that it must be his fiftieth since that first cigarette of the morning almost twenty-four hours ago.

10.

If you really want to be sure of getting caught, the thing to do is kill a policeman.

This truth applies in most places and especially in Sweden. There are plenty of unsolved murders in Swedish criminal history, but not one of them involves the murder of a policeman.

When a member of their own troop meets with misfortune, the police seem to acquire many times their usual energy. All the complaints about lack of manpower and resources stop, and suddenly it's possible to mobilize several hundred men for an investigation that would normally have occupied no more than three or four.

A man who lays hands on a policeman always gets caught. Not because the general public takes a solid stand behind the forces of law and order—as it does, for example, in England or the socialist countries—but because the police chief's entire private army suddenly knows what it wants, and, what's more, wants it very badly.

Martin Beck stood on Regeringsgatan enjoying the chilly freshness of the early morning.

He wasn't armed, but in the inside right-hand pocket of his coat he was carrying a stenciled circular from National Police Headquarters. It was a copy of a recent sociological study, and he'd found it on his desk the day before.

The police force took a very dim view of sociologists —particularly in recent years since they'd started working more and more with the activities and attitudes of policemen—and all their pronouncements were read with great suspicion by the men at the top. Perhaps the brass realized that in the long run it would prove untenable simply to insist that everyone involved in sociology was actually a communist or some other subversive.

Sociologists were capable of anything, as Superintendent Malm had recently pointed out in one of his many moments of indignation. Martin Beck, among others, was supposed to look on Malm as his superior.

Maybe Malm was right. Sociologists got all kinds of ideas. For example, they came up with the fact that you no longer needed better than a D average to get into the Police Academy, and that the average IQ of patrolmen in Stockholm had dropped to 93.

"It's a lie!" Malm had shouted. "And what's more it isn't true! And on top of that it isn't any lower than in New York!"

He'd just returned from a study tour in the States.

The report in Martin Beck's pocket revealed a

number of interesting new facts. It proved that police work wasn't a bit more dangerous than any other profession. On the contrary, most other jobs involved much greater risks. Construction workers and lumberjacks lived considerably more hazardous lives, not to mention longshoremen or taxi drivers or housewives.

But hadn't it always been generally accepted that a policeman's lot was riskier and tougher and less well paid than any other? The answer was painfully simple. Yes, but only because no other professional group suffered from such role fixation or dramatized its daily life to the same degree as did the police.

It was all supported by figures. The number of injured policemen was negligible when compared with the number of people annually mistreated by the police. And so forth.

And it didn't apply only to Stockholm. In New York, for example, an average of seven policemen were killed every year, whereas taxi drivers perished at the rate of two a month, housewives one a week, and among the unemployed the rate was one a day.

To these odious sociologists nothing was holy. There was a Swedish team that had even managed to torpedo the myth of the English bobby and reduce it to its proper proportions, namely, to the fact that the English police are not armed and therefore don't provoke violence to the same degree as certain others. Even in Denmark responsible authorities had managed to grasp this fact, and only in exceptional situations were policemen permitted to sign out weapons.

But such was not the case in Stockholm.

Martin Beck had suddenly started thinking about this study as he stood looking at Nyman's body.

And now it came to mind again. He realized that the conclusions that document drew were correct, and paradoxically enough he sensed some sort of connection between those conclusions and the murder that occupied him at the moment.

It's not dangerous to be a policeman, and in fact it's the policemen who are dangerous, and a little while ago he'd been looking down at the butchered body of a policeman.

To his surprise, the corners of his mouth started to quiver, and for a moment it felt as if he were going to sit down on the steps leading from Regeringsgatan down to Kungsgatan and burst into laughter at the whole situation.

But with the same curious logic it suddenly occurred to him that he'd better go home and get his pistol.

It was over a year since he'd even looked at it.

An empty cab came up the street from Stureplan.

Martin Beck stuck out his hand and got it to stop.

It was a yellow Volvo with a black stripe along the sides. This was a relatively recent innovation and a relaxation of the old rule that all taxicabs in Stockholm had to be black. He climbed into the front seat next to the driver.

"Köpmangatan eight," he said.

And as he said it he recognized the driver. He was one of those policemen who eke out their incomes by driving a cab during their off-duty hours. That he recognized the man was pure coincidence. Several days earlier, outside the Central Station, he'd watched two unusually maladroit patrolmen drive an initially peaceable young drunk into a belligerent rage and then lose control of themselves. The man behind the wheel was one of them.

He was about twenty-five years old and extremely garrulous.

He was probably talkative from birth, and since his regular job permitted him only an occasionally angry grunt, he made up for it here in his cab.

One of the Sanitation Department's combination sweep-and-spray trucks temporarily blocked their path. The moonlighting patrolman fretfully studied a billboard advertising Richard Attenborough's *10 Rillington Place*.

"Ten Rollington Palace, hunh?" he said in some sort of dialect. "And people want to see that kind of crap. Murder and misery and crazy people. If you ask me it's a damned shame."

Martin Beck nodded. The man, who obviously didn't recognize him, took the nod as encouragement and talked volubly on.

"But you know it's all these foreigners that make all the trouble."

Martin Beck said nothing.

"But I will say one thing, you're making a big mistake if you lump all foreigners together in one bag. The guy who drives this cab with me, he's Portuguese, for example."

"Oh?"

"Yeah, and you couldn't find a better man. He works his ass off, doesn't lie around on his butt. And can he drive! And do you know why?"

Martin Beck shook his head.

"Yeah, well, he drove a tank in Africa for four years. You know, Portugal's fighting a war of liberation down there, place called Angola. They're fighting like hell for their freedom down there, the Portuguese, but you never hear anything about it here in Sweden. This guy, the guy I'm talking about, he shot hundreds of commies those four years. And on him it really shows what a good thing the army is, and discipline and all that. He does exactly what you tell him, and he rakes in more dough than anyone else I know. And if he gets some drunk Finn bastard in the car, well, he sees to it he gets a hundred percent tip. They've got it coming, all those bums on welfare."

Just then, fortunately, the car stopped outside the building where Martin Beck lived. He told the driver to wait, let himself into the building and rode up to his apartment.

The pistol was a 7.65 mm Walther and lay in its place in a locked drawer of his desk. The clips were also where they belonged, in another locked drawer in the other room. He slipped one of them into the pistol and put the other in his right-hand coat pocket. But he had to hunt for five minutes before he could find his shoulder holster, which was lying in a pile of old neckties and T-shirts on a shelf in the closet.

Back down on the street, the effusive cop stood leaning against his yellow taxi, happily humming to himself. He held the door politely, climbed in behind the wheel and had already opened his mouth to resume his text when Martin Beck interrupted.

"Kungsholmsgatan thirty-seven, please," he said.

"But that's the . . ."

"Right, Criminal Division. Drive along Skeppsbron, please."

The driver immediately turned red in the face and didn't utter a sound the whole way there.

And that was welcome, Martin Beck thought. In spite of everything, he loved this city, and right at this place and at this time of day it was perhaps at its most beautiful. The morning sun was shining across Strömmen, and the surface of the water was smooth and calm and didn't reveal the terrible pollution that was unfortunately a fact. In his youth—in fact a lot more recently than that—you could go swimming here.

Down along the city quay lay an old cargo steamer with a tall straight stack and a black spar on the mainmast. You rarely saw them any more these days. An early Djurgård ferry was cutting through the water with a crisp little wave along its bows. He noticed that the smokestack was completely black and the name on the side was covered with white paint. But he recognized it anyway. The *Djurgård 5*.

"Do you want a receipt?" asked the driver in a stifled voice outside the doors to the police building.

"Yes, thanks."

Martin Beck went up to the offices of the Violence Division, studied some documents, made a few phone calls and did a little writing.

At the end of an hour he'd managed to put together a brief and very superficial summary of a human life. It began like this:

Stig Oscar Emil Nyman.

Born November 6, 1911, in Säffle.

Parents: Oscar Abraham Nyman, logging foreman, and Karin Maria Nyman, née Rutgersson.

Schooling: Two years elementary school in Säffle, two years grade school in Säffle, five years secondary school in Åmål.

Joined professional infantry 1928, lance corporal 1930, corporal 1931, sergeant 1933, Noncommissioned Officer's School.

And then Stig Oscar Emil Nyman had become a policeman. First as a deputy sheriff in Värmland, then as a regular police constable in Stockholm. During the depression in the thirties. His military experience was counted in his favor and led to quick promotions.

At the beginning of the Second World War he resumed his military career, was promoted and given a number of obscure special assignments. During the latter part of the war he was transferred to Karlsborg, but in 1946 he went into the reserve and one year later reappeared on the personnel roster of the Stockholm police, this time as a sergeant.

When Martin Beck went through the inspector's course in 1949, Nyman was already a deputy chief inspector and was given his first precinct command a few years later.

As a chief inspector, Nyman had at different times been chief of several precincts in the inner city. From time to time he'd been back at the old police headquarters on Agnegatan, again on assignments of a special nature.

He had spent the greater part of his life in uniform, but in spite of that was one of the men who had long been in the good graces of the highest police command.

Only circumstances had kept him from advancing even further and becoming chief for the regular metropolitan police in its entirety.

What circumstances?

Martin Beck knew the answer to that question.

At the end of the fifties, the Stockholm police department had undergone a substantial shake-up. There had been an infusion of fresh leadership and fresh air. Military thinking ceased to be so popular, and reactionary ideas were no longer necessarily an asset. The changes at headquarters spread to a certain extent out into the precincts, automatic promotion became less routine, and certain phenomena, among them the Prussian spit-and-polish of the regular police, died in the wake of the move toward greater democracy. Nyman was one of many who had watched his bridges burn before him.

It seemed to Martin Beck that the first half of the sixties had been an auspicious period in the history of the Stockholm police. Everything had seemed to be improving, common sense had been about to conquer rigidity and cliquishness, the recruiting base had been broadened, and even relations with the public had seemed to be getting better. But nationalization in 1965 had broken the positive trend. Since then, all the good prospects had been betrayed and all the good intentions laid to rest.

For Nyman, however, it came too late. It was now almost seven years since he'd had his last precinct command.

During that time he'd worked mostly on things like civil defense.

But no one had been able to take away his reputation as an expert in maintaining order, and he had been eagerly consulted as a specialist in connection with the frequent large demonstrations toward the end of the sixties.

Martin Beck scratched the back of his neck and read through the last few lines of his inconsequential notes.

Married 1945, two children in the marriage, daughter Annelotte born 1949 and son Stefan born 1956.

Early retirement due to illness 1970.

He picked up his ballpoint pen and wrote:

Died in Stockholm, April 3, 1971.

Read through the whole thing one more time. Looked at the clock. Ten minutes to seven.

He wondered how things were going for Rönn.

11.

The city woke up and yawned and stretched.

As did Gunvald Larsson. Woke up, yawned and stretched. Then he put a large hairy hand on the electric alarm clock, threw off the blanket and swung his long shaggy legs out of bed.

He put on his bathrobe and slippers and walked over to the window to check the weather. Dry, fair, thirty-sev-

en degrees. The suburb he lived in was called Boll-
mora and consisted of some high-rise apartment buildings in the woods.

Then he looked in the mirror and saw a very large
blond man, still six feet three and a half inches tall, but
weighing in these days at 230 pounds. He got a little
heavier with every year, and it was no longer pure muscle that bulged beneath the while silk robe. But he was
in good shape and felt stronger than ever, which was
saying a good deal. For several seconds he stared into
his own porcelain-blue eyes under a wrinkled brow.
Then he combed his blond hair back with his fingers,
pulled open his lips and examined his large strong teeth.

He got the morning paper from the mail slot and
went out to the kitchen to make breakfast. There he
made tea—Twining's Irish Breakfast—and toast and
boiled two eggs. He got out the butter, some Cheddar
cheese and Scottish marmalade, three different kinds.

He leafed through the paper as he ate.

Sweden had done badly in the international ice hock-
ey championships, and the managers, trainers and
players were now emphasizing their lack of sportsman-
ship by hurling accusations at each other in public.
There was also a fight going on within the Swedish
TV—the monopoly's central management was apparently doing everything it could to maintain a tight hold on
the news services of the different channels.

Censorship, thought Gunvald Larsson. With laminat-
ed plastic gloves. Typical of this meddlesome capitalist
society.

The biggest piece of news was that the readers were
being given the opportunity to christen three bear cubs
at Skansen. The results of a military study showing
forty-year-old reservists to be in better physical condition than eighteen-year-old recruits were noted with
resignation in a less prominent place. And on the cul-
ture page, where there was no risk of its being seen by
unauthorized readers, there was an article on Rhodesia.

He read it while he drank his tea and ate his eggs
and six pieces of toast.

Gunvald Larsson had never been in Rhodesia, but
many times in South Africa, Sierra Leone, Angola and

Mozambique. He'd been a seaman then, and had already known his own mind.

He finished his meal, washed the dishes and threw the paper in the trash. Since it was Saturday, he changed the sheets before making the bed. Then with great care he selected the clothes he would wear that day and laid them neatly on the bed. Removed his robe and pajamas and took a shower.

His bachelor apartment bore witness to good taste and a feeling for quality. Furniture, rugs, drapes, everything, from his white leather Italian slippers to his pivoting Normende color TV, was first class.

Gunvald Larsson was an inspector at the Violence Division in Stockholm, and higher up the ladder he would never go. As a matter of fact it was odd he hadn't been fired already. His colleagues thought him peculiar, and they almost all disliked him. He himself detested not only the men he worked with but also his own family and the upper-class background he came from. His own brothers and sisters regarded him with profound distaste. Partly as a result of his dissident views, but mostly because he was a policeman.

While showering, he wondered if he would die that day.

It was not a foreboding. He'd wondered the same thing every morning since he was eight years old and brushed his teeth before dragging himself reluctantly off to Broms School on Sturegatan.

Lennart Kollberg lay in his bed dreaming. It was not a pleasant dream. He'd had it before, and when he woke from it he'd be dripping with sweat and he'd say to Gun, "Put your arms around me, I had such an awful nightmare."

And Gun, who'd been his wife for five years, would put her arms around him and right away he'd forget everything else.

In the dream, his daughter Bodil is standing in the open window five stories above the street. He tries to run over to her, but his legs are paralyzed and she starts to fall, slowly, as if in slow motion, and she screams and stretches her arms out toward him and he fights to reach her, but his muscles won't obey him and she falls and falls, screaming all the time.

He woke up. The scream in the nightmare became the drilling buzz of the alarm clock, and when he looked up he saw Bodil sitting astride his shins.

She was reading *The Cat Trip*. She was only three and a half and she couldn't read, but Gun and he had read the story to her so many times they all knew it by heart, and he could hear Bodil whispering it to herself.

"A little old man with a big blue nose, all dressed up in calico clothes."

He turned off the alarm clock and she immediately stopped whispering and said "Hi!" in a clear high voice.

Kollberg turned his head and looked at Gun. She was still asleep, with the quilt pulled up to her nose, and her dark ruffled hair was a tiny bit damp at the temples. He put his finger to his lips.

"Shh," he whispered. "Don't wake Mommy. And don't sit on my legs, it hurts. Come up here and lie down."

He made room for her to creep down under the quilt between him and Gun. She gave him the book and arranged herself with her head in his armpit.

"Read it," she ordered.

He put the book aside.

"No, not now," he said. "Did you get the newspaper?"

She scrambled across his midriff and picked up the newspaper, which was on the floor beside the bed. He groaned, lifted her up and put her back in the bed beside him again. Then he opened the paper and started to read. He made it all the way to the foreign news on page twelve before Bodil interrupted.

"Papa?"

"Mmm."

"Josha did a big job."

"Mmm."

"He took off his diaper and put it on the wall. All over the wall."

Kollberg put down the paper and groaned again, got

out of bed and went into the children's room. Joshua, who would soon be one, was standing up in his crib and when he saw his father he let go of the railing and sat down on the pillow with a little bounce. Bodil had not exaggerated his adornment of the wall.

Kollberg picked him up under one arm, carried him into the bathroom and rinsed him off with the shower hose. Then he wrapped him in a towel and went in and put him down beside Gun, who was still asleep. He rinsed out the bedclothes and the pajamas, cleaned the crib and the wallpaper and got out a clean diaper and a fresh pair of plastic pants. Bodil scampered along beside him through it all. She was very pleased that for once his irritation was directed at Joshua instead of at herself, and she clucked and fussed officiously at her brother's bad behavior. When he'd finished cleaning up it was after seven thirty and there wasn't any point in going back to bed.

His mood improved as soon as he walked into the bedroom. Gun was awake, playing with Joshua. She had drawn up her knees and was holding him under the arms and letting him play roller coaster down her legs. Gun was an attractive and sensuous woman with both intelligence and a sense of humor. Kollberg had always imagined he would marry a woman like Gun, and though there had been quite a few women in his life, he'd been forty-one years old and had almost given up hope. She was fourteen years younger than he, and well worth waiting for. Their relationship had, from the very beginning, been uncomplicated, intimate and straightforward.

She smiled at him and held up their son, who gurgled with delight.

"Hi," she said. "Did you already give him his bath?"

Kollberg described his labors.

"Poor dear. Come lie down for a while," she said, throwing a glance at the clock. "You've got time."

Actually he didn't, but he was easy to convince. He lay down next to her with his arm under her neck, but after a while he got up again, carried Joshua in and put him down on his mattress, which was virtually dry, dressed him in a diaper and a pair of terrycloth overalls,

threw some toys in the crib and went back to Gun.
Bodil was sitting on the rug in the living room, playing
with her barn.

After a while she came in and looked at them.

"Play horsey," she said delightedly. "Daddy's the
horsey."

She tried to climb up on his back but he got rid of her
and closed the door. Then the children didn't bother
them for a long time, and when they'd made love he all
but fell asleep in his wife's arms.

When Kollberg walked across the street to his car the
clock on the Skärmarbrink subway station said eight
twenty-three. Before getting in, he turned and waved to
Gun and Bodil, who were standing in the kitchen window.

He didn't have to drive into town to get to Västberga
Avenue but could take the route through Årsta and
Enskede and avoid the worst of the traffic.

As he drove, Lennart Kollberg whistled an Irish folk-
song very loudly and very much out of tune.

The sun was shining, there was spring in the air, and
crocuses and Star-of-Bethlehem were blooming in the
gardens he passed. He was in a good mood. If he was
lucky, he'd have a short day and would be able to go
home fairly early in the afternoon. Gun was going to go
in to Arvid Nordquist's and buy something good, and
they'd have dinner after the children were in bed. After
five years of marriage their idea of a really pleasant evening was to be at home, alone, help each other make a
good dinner and then sit for a long time and eat and
drink and talk.

Kollberg was very fond of good food and drink, and
as a result had put on a little fat over the years, a little
"substance" as he preferred to call it. Anyone who
thought this fleshiness prejudicial to his agility, however, was making a serious error. He could be unexpectedly quick and lithe, and he was still in command of all
the technique and all the tricks he'd once learned in the
paratroops.

He stopped whistling and started thinking about a
problem that had occupied him a lot these last few

years. He liked his job less and less, and would really prefer to resign from the force. The problem was not easy to solve and had been complicated by the fact that a year earlier he'd been promoted to deputy chief inspector, with an appropriate raise in salary. It wasn't easy for a forty-six-year-old deputy chief inspector of police to find a different and equally well-paying job. Gun kept telling him to forget the money—the children were getting older and by and by she'd be able to go back to work. In addition to which, she'd been studying and had learned another couple of languages during the four years she'd been a housewife and would certainly draw a considerably higher salary now than she had before. Before Bodil was born, she'd been an executive secretary, and she could get a well-paid position whenever she wanted. But Kollberg didn't want her to feel she had to go back to work before she really wanted to.

On top of that he had a hard time picturing himself as a homemaker.

He was by nature somewhat lazy, but needed a certain amount of activity and change around him.

As he drove his car into the garage at Södra police station he remembered that Martin Beck had the day off.

First of all that means I'll have to stay here all day, Kollberg thought, and secondly that I won't have anyone sensible to talk to. His spirits immediately sank.

In order to cheer himself up, he started whistling again while he waited for the elevator.

12.

Kollberg hadn't even had time to take off his overcoat when the telephone rang.

"Yes, Kollberg here . . . what?"

He stood by his littered desk and stared absently out the window. The switch-over from the pleasures of private life to the ugliness of the job wasn't as easy for him as it was for some, for example Martin Beck.

"What's it about? . . . You don't? Well okay, tell them I'm coming."

Down to the car again, and this time no way to avoid the traffic.

He arrived at Kungsholmsgatan at a quarter to nine and parked in the yard. Just as Kollberg was getting out of his car, Gunvald Larsson got into his and drove away.

They nodded to each other but didn't speak. He ran into Rönn in the corridor.

"So you're here too," Rönn said.

"Yes, what's up?"

"Somebody sliced up Stig Nyman."

"Sliced up?"

"Yeah, with a bayonet," said Rönn mournfully. "At Mount Sabbath."

"I just saw Larsson. Is that where he was headed?"

Rönn nodded.

"Where's Martin?"

"He's in Melander's office."

Kollberg looked at him more closely.

"You look just about done in," he said.

"I am," said Rönn.

"Why don't you go home and go to bed?"

Rönn gave him a doleful look and walked on down the corridor. He was holding some papers in his hand and presumably had work to do.

Kollberg rapped once on the door and walked in. Martin Beck didn't even look up from his notes.

"Hi," he said.

"What's all this Rönn was talking about?"

"Here. Take a look."

He handed him two typewritten sheets of paper. Kollberg sat down on the edge of the desk and read.

"Well," said Martin Beck. "What do you think?"

"I think Rönn writes a god-awful report," said Kollberg.

But he said it quietly and seriously, and five seconds later he went on.

"This sounds unpleasant."

"Right," said Martin Beck. "I think so too."

"What'd it look like?"

"Worse than you can imagine."

Kollberg shook his head. There was nothing wrong with his imagination.

"We'd better get our hands on this guy pretty damned quick."

"Right again," said Martin Beck.

"What do we have to go on?"

"Something. We've got a few prints. Footprints, maybe some fingerprints. No one saw anything or heard anything."

"Not good," Kollberg said. "That can take time. And this guy's dangerous."

Martin Beck nodded.

Rönn came into the room after a discreet knock on the door.

"Negative so far," he said. "The fingerprints I mean."

"The fingerprints aren't worth a damn," Kollberg said.

"I've got a pretty good casting too," Rönn said. "Of a boot or a heavy work shoe." He was looking surprised.

"That's not worth a damn either," Kollberg said. "I mean, don't get me wrong. That can all be essential later on, as evidence. But right now it's a question of getting our hands on whoever slaughtered Nyman. We can tie him to the crime later on."

"That sounds illogical," Rönn said.

"Okay, but don't worry about it now. We've still got another couple of important details."

"Yes, the murder weapon," said Martin Beck thoughtfully. "An old carbine bayonet."

"And the motive," said Kollberg.

"The motive?" Rönn said.

"Of course," said Kollberg. "Revenge. It's the only conceivable motive."

"But if it's revenge . . ."

Rönn said, and left the sentence hanging.

"Then it's possible whoever stabbed Nyman is planning to take revenge on other people too," Kollberg said. "And therefore . . ."

"We have to find him fast," said Martin Beck.

"Exactly," said Kollberg. "Now what's your reasoning been?"

Rönn looked unhappily at Martin Beck, who in his turn looked out the window.

Kollberg looked at them both admonishingly.

"Wait a minute," he said. "Have you asked the question, Who was Nyman?"

"Who he was?"

Rönn seemed confused and Martin Beck said nothing.

"Right. Who was Nyman? Or more to the point, *what* was Nyman?"

"A policeman," said Martin Beck finally.

"That's not a very complete answer," Kollberg said. "Come now, you both knew him. What was Nyman?"

"A chief inspector," mumbled Rönn.

Then he blinked wearily.

"I have to make a couple of phone calls," he said evasively.

"Well?" said Kollberg, when Rönn had closed the door behind him. "What was Nyman?"

Martin Beck looked him in the eye and said, reluctantly, "He was a bad policeman."

"Wrong," said Kollberg. "Now listen. Nyman was one *hell* of a bad policeman. He was a barbaric son of a bitch of the very worst sort."

"You said it, I didn't," said Martin Beck.

"Yes. But you'll have to admit I'm right."

"I didn't know him very well."

"Don't try to sneak out of it. You knew him well enough to know that much. I realize Einar doesn't want to admit it, out of misdirected loyalty. But dammit, *you've* got to play with your cards on the table."

"All right," said Martin Beck. "The things I've heard about him aren't exactly positive. But I never really worked with him."

"Your choice of words isn't very apt," Kollberg said. "It wasn't possible to work *with* Nyman. All you could do was take orders from him and do as you were told. Of course you could give him orders too, if you happened to be in that position. And then have them sabotaged, or simply not carried out at all."

"You sound like an expert on Stig Nyman," said Martin Beck, a little acidly.

"Yes, I know some things about him the rest of you don't know. But I'll get to that later. First of all, let's get it straight that he was a bastard and a goddamned lousy policeman. Even today he'd be a disgrace to the force. For my part I'm ashamed to have been a policeman in the same city with him. And at the same time."

"In that case there are a lot of people who ought to be ashamed."

"Exactly. But there aren't so many who have the sense to be."

"And every policeman in London ought to be ashamed about Challenor."

"Wrong again," said Kollberg. "Challenor and some of his underlings were finally brought to trial, even if they did manage to do a lot of damage beforehand. And that showed that in the long run there was some limit to what the system would tolerate in the police."

Martin Beck massaged his temple thoughtfully.

"But Nyman's name has never been discredited. And why not?"

Kollberg had to answer his own question.

"Because everyone knows it's pointless to report a policeman. The general public has no legal rights vis-à-vis the police. And if you can't win a case against an ordinary patrolman, then how in the world could you win a case against a chief inspector?"

"You're exaggerating."

"Not much, Martin. Not much, and you know it as well as I do. It's just that our damned solidarity has become some kind of second nature. We're impregnated with esprit de corps."

"It's important to keep up a good front in this job," said Martin Beck. "It always has been."

"And pretty soon it'll be the only thing left."

Kollberg caught his breath before he went on.

"Okay. The police stick together. That's axiomatic. But stick together against whom?"

"The day someone answers that question . . ."

Martin Beck left the sentence hanging.

"Neither you nor I," said Kollberg with finality, "will live to see that day."

"What's all this got to do with Nyman?"

"Everything."

"In what way?"

"Nyman's dead and doesn't need to be defended any more. Whoever killed him is probably insane, a danger to himself and other people."

"And you mean we can find him in Nyman's past."

"Yes. He ought to be there. The comparison you just made wasn't so bad."

"Which comparison?"

"With Challenor."

"I don't know the truth about Challenor," said Martin Beck with a certain chill. "But maybe you do?"

"No, nobody does. But I do know a lot of people were mistreated and still more were sentenced to long prison terms because policemen perjured themselves in court. Without any reaction either from their subordinates or their superiors."

"Their superiors out of false loyalty," said Martin Beck. "And their subordinates out of fear of losing their jobs."

"Worse than that. Some of those subordinates simply thought that was the way it was supposed to be. They'd never learned any other way."

Martin Beck stood up and walked toward the window.

"Tell me what it is you know about Nyman that other people don't know," he said.

"Nyman was also in a position to give orders directly to a lot of young policemen, by and large pretty much as he pleased."

"That's a long time ago now," said Martin Beck.

"Not so long ago but what a lot of people on the force today learned most of what they know from him. Do you realize what that means? Over the years he managed to corrupt scores of young policemen. Who consequently had a warped attitude toward their jobs right from the beginning. And a lot of them out and out admired him, and hoped they could be like him some day. Just as hard and high-handed. Do you understand?"

"Yes," said Martin Beck wearily. "I see what you mean. You don't have to spell it out again and again."

He turned and looked at Kollberg.

"But that doesn't mean I believe it. Did you know Nyman?"

"Yes."

"Did you ever work under him?"

"Yes."

Martin Beck raised his eyebrows.

"And when was that, pray tell?" he said suspiciously.

"The abominable man from Säffle," said Kollberg to himself.

"What was that?"

"The abominable man from Säffle. That's what we called him."

"Where?"

"In the army. During the war. A lot of what I know I learned from Stig Nyman."

"For example?"

"That's a good question," said Kollberg absently.

Martin Beck looked at him searchingly.

"Like what, Lennart?" he asked quietly.

"Like how to cut off a pig's penis without its squealing. Like how to cut the legs off the same pig also without its squealing. Like how to gouge its eyes out. And finally how to cut it to pieces and flay it, still without a ound."

He shivered.

"Do you know how?" he said.

Martin Beck shook his head.

"It's easy. You start by cutting out its tongue."

Kollberg looked out through the window, up toward the cold blue sky above the roofs on the other side of the street.

"Oh, he taught me a great deal. How to cut a sheep's throat with piano wire before it has a chance to bleat. How to handle a full-grown wildcat you're locked up in a closet with. The way to bellow when you charge a cow and stick a bayonet in its belly. And what happens if you don't bellow properly. Fill your pack with bricks and climb the ladder on the training tower. Fifty times up and fifty times down. You weren't allowed to kill the wildcat, by the way, it had to be used again. Know what you did?"

"No."

"You nailed it to the wall with your sheath knife. Through its skin."

"You were a paratrooper, weren't you?"

"Yes. And Nyman was my instructor in hand-to-hand combat. Among other things. He taught me how it feels to lie buried in the guts of freshly slaughtered animals, and he taught me to eat my own vomit when I'd thrown up inside a gas mask, and my own shit to avoid leaving a track."

"What was his rank?"

"He was a sergeant. A lot of the things he taught couldn't be learned in the classroom. For example how to break an arm or a leg or crush a larynx or press eyes out with your thumbs. You can only learn that by doing it, on something that's alive. Sheep and pigs were convenient. We also tested different kinds of ammunition on live animals, particularly pigs, and by God there wasn't any crap about anesthetizing them first like they do these days."

"Was that normal training?"

"I don't know. For that matter, what do you mean? Can you ever call that sort of thing *normal?*"

"Maybe not."

"But even if you suppose that for some ridiculous reason all of that was necessary, it wasn't necessary to do it with joy and pride."

"No. But Nyman did, you mean?"

"I'll say. And he taught his craft to a lot of kids. To brag about brutality, to enjoy cruelty. Some people have a gift for it."

"In other words he was a sadist."

"In the highest degree. He called it 'hardness' himself. He was naturally hard. And for a real man, the only thing that mattered was being hard. Physically and mentally. He always encouraged bullying. Said it was part of a soldier's education."

"That doesn't necessarily make him a sadist."

"He exposed himself in a lot of ways. He was a tremendous disciplinarian. Maintaining discipline is one thing, but dealing out your own punishments is another. Nyman nailed someone or several people every day, for trifles. A lost button, that sort of thing. And the men he caught always had to choose."

"Between what?"

"A report or a beating. A report meant three days in the brig and a black mark on your military record. So most people chose the beating."

"What did that involve?"

"I took the bait just once. I was late back to camp one Saturday night. Climbed over the fence. Nyman caught me, of course. And I chose the beating. What it involved in my case was that I stood at attention with a bar of soap in my mouth while he broke two of my ribs with his fists. Then he treated me to a cup of coffee and a piece of cake and told me he thought I could probably get to be really hard, a real soldier."

"And then?"

"As soon as the war was over I saw to it that I got drummed out of the army, quickly and neatly. Then I came here and became a cop. And one of the first people I saw was Nyman. He was already a sergeant."

"And you mean to say he went on using the same methods as a policeman?"

"Maybe not the same. He could hardly get away with that. But he's probably committed hundreds of outrages of one kind and another. Toward his subordinates and toward arrestees. I've heard various stories over the years."

"He must have been reported now and then," said Martin Beck thoughtfully.

"I'm sure. But because of our esprit de corps I'm also sure that none of those reports are still around. They all wound up in wastepaper baskets naturally—most of them no doubt dismissed out of hand. So we won't find out anything around here."

Martin Beck suddenly had a thought.

"But the Justice Department Ombudsman," he said. "Some of the people who really were mistreated must have lodged complaints with the J.O."

"To no avail," Kollberg said. "A man like Nyman always sees to it that there are policemen ready to take an oath that he hadn't done anything. Young fellows, whose jobs would be hell if they refused. And the kind of men who are already so indoctrinated they figure they're only doing what loyalty demands. No one outside the force can get at a chief inspector."

"True enough," said Martin Beck. "But the J.O. doesn't throw away his reports, even when they don't lead to any action. They're filed away, and they're still there."

"That's an idea," said Kollberg slowly. "Not a bad idea at all. You have your moments."

He thought about it for a while.

"Best of all would be if we had a civilian review board that recorded every case of police misconduct. Unfortunately, there is no such thing in this country. But maybe the J.O. can give us something."

"And the murder weapon," Martin Beck said. "A carbine bayonet must come from the army. Not everybody has a chance to get his hands on one of those. I'll put Rönn on that detail."

"Yes, do. And then take Rönn with you and go to the J.O.'s archive."

"What are you planning to do?"

"Actually I'm thinking of going over and having a look at Nyman," Kollberg said. "Larsson's there, of course, but I don't care. I'm doing it mostly for my own sake, want to see how I react. Maybe I'll get sick, but at least no one can make me eat my vomit."

Martin Beck no longer looked quite so tired. He straightened up.

"Lennart?"

"Yeah?"

"What was it you called him? The abominable man from Säffle?"

"That's right. He came from Säffle, and he never stopped telling us about it. Men from Säffle were really hard, he'd say. Real men. And like I said he was certainly abominable. One of the most sadistic men I've ever met."

Martin looked at him for a long time.

"Maybe you're right," he said.

"There's a chance. Good luck. I hope you find something."

Again Martin Beck had an indefinable sense of danger.

"I think this is going to be a rough day."

"Yes," said Kollberg. "It's got all the makings. Do you feel a little cured of your loyalty?"

"I think so."

"Remember Nyman doesn't need any gratuitous loyalty any more. Which reminds me, by the way, that he had an unswervingly faithful sidekick all these years. Guy named Hult. He ought to be a captain by now, if he's still around. Somebody ought to talk to him."

Martin Beck nodded.

Rönn scratched at the door and came in. He was unsteady on his feet and looked all done in from exhaustion. His eyes were red and sticky from the lack of sleep.

"What do we do now?" he said.

"We've got a lot of work in front of us. Can you make it?"

"Well yes, I guess I can," Rönn said, and stifled a yawn.

13.

Martin Beck had no trouble gathering biographical data on the man Kollberg described as Nyman's faithful sidekick. His name was Harald Hult, and he'd been a policeman all his adult life. His career was easily followed in the department's own archives.

He'd started out, at nineteen, as a deputy constable in Falun and was now a captain. As far as Martin Beck could see, Hult and Nyman had first served together in 1936 and 1937 when they'd been patrolmen in the same Stockholm precinct. In the middle of the forties they'd been reunited in another downtown precinct. The somewhat younger Nyman was by then a lieutenant, while Hult was still only a patrolman.

During the fifties and sixties, Hult began little by little to advance and on several different occasions served under Nyman. Presumably, Nyman had been allowed to choose the assistants he needed for his special assignments, and Hult had quite clearly been one of his favorites. If Nyman was the kind of man Kollberg said he was, and there was no reason to doubt it, then any man who'd been his "unswervingly faithful sidekick" ought to be a very interesting psychological phenomenon.

Martin Beck started to be curious about Harald Hult and decided to take Kollberg's advice and look him up. He called and made sure the man was at home before taking a taxi to the specified address on Reimersholme.

Hult lived on the northern tip of the island, in one of the apartment houses facing the Långholm Channel. The building stood on a high point of land, and on the other side of the street, which stopped abruptly in front of the last apartment house in the row, the ground sloped steeply down to the water.

The area looked pretty much the way it had at the end of the thirties when it was built, and owing to its location there was no through traffic. Reimersholme was a fairly small island, with only one bridge in and out, and the buildings were few and far between. A third of its area was occupied by the old alcohol plant and various other old factories and warehouses. There were generous gardens and grounds between the apartment houses, and the shore along Långholm Bay had been left in peace, so that the natural vegetation—alder and aspen and weeping willow—grew rank and lush right down to the water.

Captain Harald Hult lived alone in a two-room apartment on the second floor. It was clean and neat and somehow so tidy it seemed desolate. Almost, thought Martin Beck, as if it were unoccupied.

Hult himself looked to be about sixty, a large, heavy man with a strong chin and expressionless gray eyes.

They sat down by a low, varnished table near the window. The tabletop was bare, and nothing stood on the windowsill. There was, in fact, a general lack of ordinary personal possessions. There didn't seem to be any paper in the apartment, for example, not even so much as a newspaper, and the only books he could discover were the three parts of the telephone directory, standing neatly on a little shelf in the front hall.

Martin Beck unbuttoned his jacket and loosened his tie a bit. Then he took out his pack of Floridas and a box of matches and started looking around for an ashtray.

Hult followed his glance.

"I don't smoke," he said. "I don't think I've ever owned an ashtray."

He got a white saucer from the kitchen cabinet.

"Can I get you something . . . ?" he asked before sitting down again. "I've already had my coffee, but I can make some more."

Martin Beck shook his head. He noticed that Hult was a trifle uncertain about how to address him, whether or not he ought to say "sir" to the head of the National Homicide Squad. That showed he was a man of the old school, where rank and discipline had been taken for granted. Although Hult had the day off, he was wearing his uniform trousers, a light blue shirt and a tie.

"Haven't you got the day off?" Martin Beck asked.

"I wear my uniform most of the time," Hult said tonelessly. "I prefer it."

"Nice place you've got," said Martin Beck, glancing out the window at the view.

"Yes," Hult said. "I guess so. Though it's pretty lonely."

He put his large, meaty hands on the table in front of him as if they'd been a pair of clubs, and stared at them.

"I'm a widower. My wife died three years ago. Cancer. Since then it's been kind of dull."

Hult didn't smoke and didn't drink. He certainly never read a book and probably not the papers either. Martin Beck could picture him sitting passively in front of the TV while the darkness gathered outside.

"What's it all about?"

"Stig Nyman is dead."

There was virtually no reaction at all. The man threw a vacant look at his visitor.

"Oh?"

"I suppose you knew already."

"No. But it's hardly unexpected. Stig was sick. His body failed him."

He looked back at his clublike fists, as if wondering how long it would be before his own body betrayed him.

"Did you know Stig?" he asked after a moment.

"Not very well," Martin Beck said. "About as well as I know you."

"That's not very well. We've only met a couple of times, sir, you and I."

And then he dropped the "sir" and went on in a more familiar tone.

"I've always been in the regular police. Never had much chance to hang around with you people at Criminal."

"On the other hand you knew Nyman pretty well, didn't you?"

"Yes. We worked together for years."

"And what did you think of him?"

"He was a very good man."

"I've heard the opposite."

"Who from?"

"Different places."

"In that case it's wrong. Stig Nyman was a very good man. That's all I can tell you."

"Oh," said Martin Beck. "I'm sure you can fill out the picture a bit."

"No. In what way?"

"You know perfectly well, for example, that a lot of people criticized him. That there were people who didn't like him."

"No, I don't know anything about that."

"Really? I know, for example, that Nyman had his own particular methods."

"He was good," Hult repeated monotonously. "Very competent. A real man, and the best boss you could imagine."

"But he took rather strong measures now and then?"

"Who says so? Someone who's trying to run him down now that he's dead, of course. If anyone says anything like that, then it's a lie."

"But he was inclined to be pretty hard, wasn't he?"

"Never more than the situation required. Anything else is slander."

"But you knew there were quite a lot of complaints about Nyman?"

"No, I didn't know."

"Let's put it this way—I know you knew. You worked directly under him."

"Just lies, to blacken the name of a fine and capable policeman."

"There are people who think Nyman wasn't a fine policeman at all."

"In that case they don't know what they're talking about."

"But you do."

"Yes, I do. Stig Nyman was the best commander I ever had."

"There are people who say that you're not a particularly good policeman either."

"Maybe not. I've never had a bad mark on my record, but maybe not anyway. Trying to run down Stig Nyman is another story completely. And if anyone does it in my presence I'll . . ."

"You'll what?"

"I'll shut their mouths."

"How?"

"That's my business. I'm an old hand. I know this job. I learned it from the bottom up."

"From Stig Nyman?"

Hult looked back at his hands.

"Yes. I guess you could say that. He taught me a lot."

"How to commit perjury, for example? How to copy each other's reports so everything'll jibe, even if every word's a lie? How to rough people up in their cells? Where the best places are to park in peace and quiet if you want to give some poor bastard a little extra going over on the way from the precinct to Criminal?"

"I've never heard of that kind of thing."

"No?"

"No."

"Not even *heard* of it?"

"No. In any case not in connection with Nyman."

"And you've never helped cut down strikers? Back in the days when the police carried sabers? And on Nyman's orders?"

"No."

"Or ride down student protesters? Or club unarmed schoolchildren at demonstrations? Still according to Nyman's instructions?"

Hult didn't move, just looked calmly at Martin Beck.

"No, I've never done any of that."

"How long have you been a policeman?"

"For forty years."

"And how long have you known Nyman?"

"Since the middle of the thirties."

Martin Beck shrugged his shoulders.

"It seems odd," he said dispassionately, "that you know nothing at all about any of the things I've mentioned. Stig Nyman was supposed to be an expert on maintaining order."

"Not only supposed to be. He was the best."

"And among other things he wrote studies on how the police should conduct themselves in demonstrations, strikes and riots. Studies where he recommended just such things as shock attacks with drawn sabers. Later on, when the sabers had disappeared, with nightsticks. He also suggested that motorcycle police should drive into crowds to break them up."

"I've never seen anything like that."

"No. That tactic was forbidden. They decided there was too much risk that the policemen would fall off their machines and injure themselves."

"I don't know anything about it."

"No, so you said. Nyman also had views on how to use tear gas and water cannons. Views he expressed officially and in his capacity as expert."

"All I know is that Stig Nyman never used more force than necessity required."

"Personally?"

"And he didn't let his subordinates do so either."

"In other words he was always right? Always stuck to the regulations, I mean."

"Yes."

"And no one had cause to complain?"

"No."

"And still it did happen that people reported Nyman for misconduct," Martin Beck pointed out.

"Then their reports were fabrications."

Martin Beck stood up and paced a few steps back and forth.

"There's one thing I haven't told you," he said. "But I'll tell you now."

"There's something I'd like to say too," Hult said.

"What is it?"

The man sat motionless, but his eyes sought out the window.

"I don't have very much to do when I'm off work," he said. "Like I said before, it's been kind of dull since Maja died. I sit here by the window a lot and count the cars that go by. There aren't an awful lot on a street like this. So I mostly sit and think."

He stopped talking and Martin Beck waited.

"I don't have much to think about," he said, "except the way my own life's been. Forty years in uniform in this city. How many times have people puked on me? How many times have people spit at me and stuck their tongues out at me and called me a pig or a swine or a murderer? How many suicides have I cleaned up? How many hours of unpaid overtime have I put in? All my life I've worked like a dog in order to try to maintain a little law and order, so respectable people could live in peace, so decent women wouldn't get raped, so every single shop window wouldn't get broken and every damn thing in sight get stolen. I've handled bodies so rotten that big white worms fell out of my cuffs at night when I got home and sat down to eat. I've changed the diapers on kids whose mothers had the d.t.'s. I've looked for lost kittens and I've stepped into knife fights. The whole time it's only been getting worse and worse —more and more violence and blood and more and more people running us down. They always say us policemen are supposed to protect society, sometimes against working stiffs and sometimes against students, sometimes against Nazis and sometimes against Communists. And now there's hardly anything left to protect any more. But you put up with it, because the morale on the force has been good. And if there'd been more men like Stig Nyman, then things wouldn't be the way they are today. So anyone who wants to hear a lot of old women's gossip about his buddies, he doesn't need to come to me."

He lifted his hands an inch or so from the table and let them fall back again with a heavy smack.

"Yes, well, that turned out to be a real speech," he said. "Nice to get it said. You've been a patrolman yourself, haven't you?"

Martin Beck nodded.

"When?"

"Over twenty years ago. After the war."

"Yes," Hult said. "Those were the days."

The apology was apparently over. Martin Beck cleared his throat.

"Now for what I wanted to say. Nyman didn't die of his illness. He was murdered. We think whoever killed him was after revenge. It's possible the man in question may have other people on his list."

Hult stood up and went out in the hall. He took down the jacket to his uniform and put it on. Then he tightened the shoulder belt and adjusted his holster.

"When I came here, it was to ask a particular question," said Martin Beck. "Who could have hated Stig Nyman enough to want to kill him?"

"No one. Now I have to go."

"Where to?"

"To work," Hult said, and held open the door.

14.

Einar Rönn sat with his elbows on the tabletop and his head in his hands and read. He was so tired that letters and words and whole lines kept flowing together or sagging or hopping out of place, upward sometimes and sometimes down, just the way they often did on his aging Remington whenever he really tried to type something perfectly with no mistakes. He yawned and blinked and cleaned his glasses and started over from the beginning.

The text before him was handwritten on a piece of brown paper bag from a state liquor store, and despite the misspellings and the writer's shaky hand, it gave the impression of having been written with patience and industry.

To His Honor The Justise Department Ombusman in Stockholm

On the second of February this year I got drunk I had got my pay and boght a fith of vodka. I remember I was sitting singing down by the Djurgård ferry and then a police car came up and three Policemen just yung kids I am old enough to be there father althogh I would want my children to be Human Beings not Pigs like that if I had any got out and took away my bottel which there was some left in and dragged me to a gray VW bus and there was another Policeman with strips on his slieve and he grabbed me by the hair and when the others had threw me in the vehicle he hit my face several times against the floor and it started bleeding thogh I felt nothing at the time. Then I sat in a cell with bars and then came a big man and abserved me thrugh the door he laffed at my misery and told another Policeman to unlock the door and then he took of his coat which there was a broad strip on the sleive and rolled up his shirt-sleives and then he came in to the cell and shouted that I should stand at attension

70

*and that I had called the Police Nastards which maybe
I had and I do not know wether he thot I ment Bas-
tards or Nazis and I was sober then and he punched
me in my stomach and another place I wont right and
I fell down and then he kicked me in the abdomen
and other places and afterwards he left and first he sed
now I knew what happened to people who fooled with
the Police. The subsequent morning, I was released
and then I asked who the Policeman was with the strip
who kicked and shouted and punched but they said I
better forget about that and I better go befor they
changed there mind and give me a real working over.
But a nother one who's name was Vilford and was
from the city of Gothenburg said that the one who
kicked and shouted and hit me was named Chief Inspector Nyman and I would be well advised to keep
my mouth shut. I have thought about this for several
days and thought I am a ordanary common worker
and I did not do anything bad except sing and be
under the influance of Alcohol but I want to have my
Rights because persons who kick and beat a poor
drunk man who has always worked all his life shold
not be a Policeman because he is not a proper person.
I swear that this is true...*

> *Respectfully
> John Bertilsson, laborer*

*It was a friend of mine at my work who is called the
Proffessor who said I should write this and I could get
justise in this way which is now common.*

OFFICIAL REMARKS: *The officer named in the complaint is Chief Inspector Stig Oscar Nyman. He knows
nothing of the case. Emergency Squad commander,
Lieutenant Harald Hult, certifies the apprehension of
the complainant Bertilsson, who is a notorious trou-
blemaker and alcoholic. No violence was employed in
the apprehension of Bertilsson nor later in the detention cell. Chief Inspector Nyman was not even on
duty at the time. Three patrolmen then on duty testify
that no violence was employed against Bertilsson. This
man shows alcoholic brain damage and is often delin-
quent. He is in the habit of bursting out with unfound-*

*ed accusations against the patrolmen who are forced
to take action against him.*

A red stamp completed the document: NO ACTION.

Rönn sighed gloomily and wrote down the complainant's name in his notebook. The woman who'd been
stuck with this extra Saturday overtime slammed the file
drawers demonstratively.

So far she'd found seven complaints that had to do
with Nyman in one way or another.

One was now out of the way, and six remained. Rönn
took them in order.

The next letter was correctly addressed and neatly
typed on heavy linen paper. The body of the letter ran
as follows:

> *On the afternoon of Saturday the 14th of this
> month, I was on the sidewalk outside the entrance to
> number 15 Pontonjärgatan together with my five-
> year-old daughter.*
>
> *We were waiting for my wife, who was visiting an
> invalid in the building. To pass the time, we were
> playing tag on the sidewalk. There was no one on the
> street as far as I can remember. It was, as I said, a
> Saturday afternoon and the stores were closed. Conse-
> quently I have no witnesses to what occurred.*
>
> *I had tagged my daughter, lifted her up in the air
> and had just put her down on the sidewalk when I dis-
> covered that a police car had stopped at the curb. Two
> patrolmen got out of the car and came up to me. One
> of them immediately grabbed my arm and said, "What
> are you doing to the kid, you son of a bitch?" (To be
> fair, I should add that I was casually dressed in khaki
> pants, windbreaker and a cap, all of it clean and fairly
> new to be sure, but may nevertheless have looked
> shabby to the patrolman in question.) I was too aston-
> ished to say anything right away. The other patrolman
> took my daughter by the hand and told her to go find
> her mother. I explained that I was her father. One of
> the patrolmen then twisted my arm behind my back,
> which was extremely painful, and shoved me into the
> back seat of the patrol car. On the way to the station,
> one of them hit me with his fist in the chest, side and*

stomach, all the time calling me names like "child molester" and "dirty old bastard" and so forth.

Once at the station, they locked me in a cell. A while later the door opened and Chief Inspector Stig Nyman (I didn't know who it was at the time, but found out later) came into the cell. "Are you the guy who chases little girls? I'll take that out of you," he said, and hit me so hard in the stomach that I doubled up. As soon as I'd caught my breath I told him I was the girl's father and he kneed me in the groin. He continued to beat me until someone came and told him my wife and daughter were there. As soon as the Chief Inspector understood that I had been telling the truth, he told me to go, without apologizing or in any way attempting to explain his behavior.

I wish hereby to draw your attention to the events described and to request that Chief Inspector Nyman and the two patrolmen be held to account for this mistreatment of a completely innocent citizen.

Sture Magnusson, engineer

OFFICIAL REMARKS: *Chief Inspector Nyman has no recollection of the complainant. Patrolmen Ström and Rosenkvist claim to have apprehended the complainant on the grounds that he acted oddly and threatened the child. They applied no more force than was required to move Magnusson into and out of the car. None of the five patrolmen who were in the precinct station at the time admits to having witnessed any mistreatment of the complainant. Nor did any of them notice that Chief Inspector Nyman entered the detention cell and believe they can say he did not. No action.*

Rönn put the paper to one side, made a note in his notebook and went on to the next complaint.

The Justice Department Ombudsman
Stockholm

Last Friday, October 18th, I attended a party at the home of a good friend on Östermalmsgatan. At about ten o'clock P.M. another friend of mine and I called a taxi and left the party to go to my apartment. We were standing in the entranceway, waiting for the taxi, when two policemen came walking down the other side of the street. They crossed the street and came up to us and asked us if we lived in the building. We answered that we did not. "Then move along, don't hang around here," they said. We said that we were waiting for a taxi and stayed where we were. The policemen then grabbed hold of us rather brusquely and pushed us out of the entranceway and told us to keep moving. But we wanted the taxi we'd ordered, and said so. The two patrolmen first tried to force us to move on by pushing us in front of them, and when we protested, one of them took out his nightstick and started to hit my friend with it. I tried to protect my friend and so I too received several blows. Both of them now had their nightsticks out and were pummeling us as hard as they could. I kept hoping the taxi would come so we would be able to get away, but it didn't come and finally my friend yelled, "They'll beat us to death, we'd better get out of here." We then ran up to Karlavägen where we took a bus to my apartment. We were both of us black and blue and my right wrist started to swell when we got home. It was badly bruised and discolored. We decided to report the incident at the police station where we supposed the two patrolmen had come from and took a taxi there. The two policemen were nowhere to be seen, but we were able to speak to a chief inspector whose name was Nyman. We were told to wait until the patrolmen came in, which they did at one o'clock. Then all four of us, the two policemen and the two of us, were called into Inspector Nyman's office and we repeated our story of what had happened. Nyman asked the policemen if it was true and they denied it. The Chief Inspector naturally believed them and told us we had better watch out for trying to blacken the names of honest hard-working policemen, and that it would go hard with us if we did it again. Then he told us to get out.

  I now wonder if Chief Inspector Nyman acted properly. What I have described is absolutely true, as my friend can testify. We were not drunk. On Monday I showed my hand to our doctor at work and he wrote the enclosed certification. We never found out *the names of the two patrolmen, but we would recognize them.*

> *Respectfully,*
> *Olof Johansson*

Rönn didn't understand all the terms in the doctor's report, but it appeared that the hand and wrist were swollen from an exudation of fluid, that the swelling would have to be punctured if it didn't go down by itself, and that the patient, who was a typographer, should refrain from working until one or the other had occurred.

Then he read through the official comment.

> *Chief Inspector Stig O. Nyman recalls the incident. He claims he had no reason to doubt the testimony of Patrolman Bergman and Sjögren, as they had always shown themselves to be honest and conscientious. Patrolmen Bergman and Sjögren deny that they used their nightsticks against the complainant and his companion, who, the patrolmen claim, were defiant and unruly. They gave the impression of being inebriated, and Patrolman Sjögren claims to have noticed a strong smell of alcohol from at least one of the men. No action.*

The woman had stopped slamming file drawers and came over to Rönn.

"I can't find any more from that year involving this Inspector Nyman. So unless I go further back . . ."

"No, that's okay, just bring me the ones you find," said Rönn cryptically.

"Will you be much longer?"

"I'll be done in a minute, just want to look through these," he said, and the woman's steps moved away behind him.

He took off his glasses and polished them before he went on reading.

> *The undersigned is a widow, employed, and the sole support of one child. The child is four years old and stays at a day-care center while I am at work. My*

nerves and health have been bad ever since my husband was killed in an automobile accident one year ago.

Last Monday I went to work as usual after leaving my daughter at the day-care center. Something happened at my place of work during the afternoon which I won't go into here, but it left me very upset. The staff doctor, who is aware of the state of my nerves, gave me a hypo and sent me home in a taxi. When I got home it didn't seem to me the sedative was having any effect, so I took two tranquillizers. I then went to get my daughter from the day-care center. When I'd gone two blocks, a police car stopped and two policemen got out and shoved me into the back seat. I was feeling a little drowsy from the medicine and it's possible I staggered a little on the street, because I gathered from the policemen's scornful way of treating me that they thought I was drunk. I tried to explain to them what the situation was and that I had to pick up my child, but they only made fun of me.

At the police station I was taken to the chief who wouldn't listen to me either but ordered them to put me in a cell "to sleep it off."

There was a buzzer in the cell and I rang it again and again but no one came. I shouted and yelled that someone had to take care of my child, but no one paid any attention. The day-care center closes at six o'clock and the staff people naturally get uneasy if you haven't picked up your child by then. It was five thirty when I was locked up.

I tried to attract someone's attention in order to be allowed to call the day-care center and see to it that my child was taken care of. I was very upset about this.

I wasn't let out until ten o'clock that night, and by that time I was beside myself with worry and desperation. I have not yet recovered and am now on sick leave.

The woman who wrote the letter had included her own address and those of the day-care center, her place of work, her doctor, and the police station to which she'd been taken.

The comment on the back of the letter read as follows:

The designated radio patrolmen are Hans Lennart Svensson and Göran Broström. They say they acted in good faith, as the woman appeared to be highly inebriated. Chief Inspector Stig Oscar Nyman claims the woman was so far gone she could not make herself understood. No action.

Rönn put the letter down and sighed. He remembered reading in an interview with the National Chief of Police that of 742 complaints about police misconduct received by the Ombudsman over a period of three years, only one had been delivered to the public prosecutor for legal action.

A man might well wonder what that went to prove, Rönn thought.

That the National Chief of Police publicized the fact only demonstrated what Rönn already knew about that gentleman's intellectual gifts.

The next document was brief, penciled in block letters on a lined sheet from a spiral notebook.

Dear J.O.,

Last Friday I got drunk and there's nothing funny about that since I've got drunk before and when the police take me in I sleep it off in the stasion. I'm a peaceful man and don't make no trouble. So now last Friday they took me in and I thought I'd get to bed down in a cell like usual, but I was sadly mistaken because a policeman I seen there before came into the cell and started to give me a beating. I was surprised because I hadn't done nothing and this policeman he cursed and raised hell, I'm sure he's the chief at the stasion, and beat me and shouted so now I want to report this police chief so he won't do it again. He is a big tall man and has a gold stripe on his jacket.

Respectfully
Joel Johansson

OFFICIAL REMARKS: *The complainant is known for countless drinking offenses, not only in the precinct in question. The policeman referred to would appear to be Inspector Stig Nyman. He claims he has never seen the complainant, whose name is however familiar to him. Inspector Nyman dismisses the suggestion that he or anyone else mistreated the complainant in his cell. No action.*

Rönn made a note in his notebook and hoped he'd be able to decipher his own handwriting. Before getting down to the two remaining complaints, he took off his glasses and rubbed his aching eyes. Then he blinked several times and read on.

My husband was born in Hungary and does not write Swedish well, so I, his wife, am writing this instead. My husband has suffered from epilepsy for many years and is now retired due to his illness. Because of his illness he sometimes has attacks and then he falls down, although he usually knows in advance when they are coming so he can stay at home, but sometimes he can't tell in advance and then it can happen anywhere. He gets medicine from his doctor, and after all these years we've been married I know how to take care of him. I want to say that there is one thing my husband never does and never's done and that is to drink. He would rather die than taste strong drink.

Now my husband and I would like to report something that happened to him last Sunday when he was coming home from the subway. He had been out to see a soccer match. Then when he was sitting on the subway train he could tell he was going to have an attack and he hurried up to get home quick and as he was walking along he fell down and the next thing he knew he was lying on a bed in a prison. By now he was better but he needed his medicine and wanted to get home to me, his wife. He had to stay there for several hours before the police let him go because all the time they thought he was drunk which he absolutely was not since he never drinks a drop. When they let him out they made him go in to see the Inspector himself and he tells him that he is sick and not drunk, but

*the Inspector didn't want to understand at all and says
my husband is lying and he'd better stay sober in the
future and that he has had enough of drunken foreigners
which my husband is of course. But he can't help
it if he speaks Swedish so badly. Then my husband
told the Inspector that he never drinks and wether the
Inspector misunderstood or whatever anyway he got
mad and knocked my husband down on the floor and
then picked him up and threw him out of the room.
Then my husband got to come home, and of course I
was terribly worried all evening and called all the hospitals
but how was I to imagine the police would take a
sick man and throw him into jail and then beat him up
as if he was the worst criminal.*

*Now my daughter tells me, we have a daughter
though she is married, that we can report this to Your
Honor. When my husband got home it was past midnight
although the game was over at seven o'clock.*

*Respectfully
Ester Nagy*

OFFICIAL REMARKS: *The chief inspector named in
the complaint, Stig Oscar Nyman, says he remembers
the man, who was treated well and sent home as
quickly as possible. Patrolmen Lars Ivar Ivarsson and
Sten Holmgren, who brought Nagy in, claim that
Nagy gave the impression of being dazed by alcohol
or narcotics. No action.*

The final petition appeared also to be the most interesting, in that it had been written by a policeman.

*The Office of the Parliamentary Ombudsman
Västra Trädgårdsgatan 4
Box 16327
Stockholm 16
Sir,*

*I hereby respectfully request that the Justice Department
Ombudsman take up for review and reconsideration
my petitions of September 1, 1961, and December
31, 1962, regarding official misconduct by*

*Chief Inspector of Police Stig Oscar Nyman and Po-
lice Sergeant Harald Hult.*

Respectfully,

Åke Reinhold Eriksson, Patrolman

"Oh, him," said Rönn to himself.

He went on to study the remarks, which for once were longer than the petition itself.

*In view of the meticulousness with which the indi-
cated petitions were previously investigated, and considering the length of time that has passed since the
presumed occurrence of the events and incidents set
forth therein, as well as with regard to the large
number of petitions submitted by the suppliant over
the past few years, I do not find that cause for reconsideration exists, particularly inasmuch as the new
facts and fresh proofs that might corroborate the peti-
tioner's previous assertions and affirmations have not
to my knowledge been manifested, and do therefore
determine that the suppliant's petition be left without
action or proceeding.*

Rönn shook his head and wondered if he had read that correctly. Probably not. In any case the signature was illegible, and, what's more, he knew something about the case of Patrolman Eriksson.

More than ever now, the writing had a tendency to flow together and distort, and when the woman put a new bundle of documents by his right elbow, he made a gesture as if to ward them off.

"Shall I go further back in time?" she asked pertly. "Do you want what there is on this man Hult too? And on yourself?"

"I'd rather not," Rönn said meekly. "I'll just take the names on these latest ones, and then we can go. Both of us."

He blinked and scribbled some more in his notebook.

"I can get out Ullholm's petitions too," the woman said sarcastically. "If you really want."

Ullholm was an inspector in Solna, notorious for a greater degree of cantankerousness and a greater number of written complaints to every imaginable authority than anyone else on the force.

Rönn drooped over the table and shook his head dejectedly.

15.

On his way to Mount Sabbath, Lennart Kollberg suddenly remembered that he hadn't paid the application fee for a correspondence chess tournament he wanted to enter. The deadline was Monday, so he stopped the car by Vasa Park and went into the post office across from Tennstopet.

When he'd filled in the money order, he stepped obediently into line and waited his turn.

In front of him was a man in a goatskin coat and a fur hat. As always when Kollberg stood in line, he found himself behind a person with about two dozen complicated errands. The man was holding a thick packet of postal orders and notices and correspondence in his hand.

Kollberg shrugged his massive shoulders, sighed and waited. A small piece of paper suddenly loosened from the man's sheaf of papers and fluttered to the floor. A stamp. Kollberg bent down and picked it up. Then touched the man on the shoulder.

"You dropped this."

The man turned his head and looked at Kollberg with brown eyes that registered surprise, recognition and antipathy, in that order.

"You dropped this," Kollberg repeated.

"It's too damned much," the man said slowly, "when you can't even drop a postage stamp but what the police come sticking their filthy noses in."

Kollberg held out the stamp.

"Keep it," the man said, and turned away.

Shortly afterward he finished his postal chores and walked away without so much as a glance at Kollberg.

The episode bewildered him. It was probably some

kind of a joke, but on the other hand the man hadn't seemed the least bit jocular. Since Kollberg was a poor physiognomist and often failed to place faces he ought to have recognized, there was nothing remarkable in the fact that the other man had recognized him while Kollberg, for his part, hadn't the vaguest idea who it was he'd spoken to.

He sent off his application fee.

Then he looked suspiciously at the stamp. It was rather pretty, with a picture of a bird. It belonged to a series of newly released stamps which, if he understood the thing correctly, guaranteed that letters bearing them would be conveyed with special sluggishness. The kind of subtlety so typical of the post office.

No, he thought, the post office really functioned pretty well and a person shouldn't grumble, not now that it had apparently recovered from the after-effects of the zip code system introduced a few years before.

Still lost in thought about the peculiarities of life, he drove on to the hospital.

The murder pavilion was still carefully cordoned off and nothing in particular had been altered in Nyman's room.

Gunvald Larsson was there, of course.

Kollberg and Gunvald Larsson did not have any special weakness for one another. The people with a weakness for Gunvald Larsson, could, for that matter, be counted on the index finger of one hand, and as easily named—Rönn.

The thought that they would be forced to work together was extremely uninviting to both Kollberg and Gunvald Larsson. At the moment there didn't seem to be any great risk—it was merely that circumstances had brought them together in the same room.

The circumstances were Nyman, whose appearance was so disagreeable that Kollberg felt called upon to deliver himself of an "Ugh!"

Gunvald Larsson grimaced in reluctant agreement.

"Did you know him?" he said.

Kollberg nodded.

"So did I. He was one of the most glorious assholes

ever to grace this department. But I never had to work with him much, thank God."

Gunvald Larsson had never really served in the regular police, only belonged to it *pro forma* for a time. Before becoming a policeman he'd been a ship's officer, first in the navy and then in the merchant marine. So unlike Kollberg and Martin Beck, he had not come up the so-called hard way.

"How's the investigation going here?"

"I don't think we'll get anything beyond what's already obvious," said Gunvald Larsson. "Some crazy bastard came in through that window and butchered him. In cold blood."

Kollberg nodded.

"But that bayonet interests me," Gunvald Larsson muttered, more or less to himself. "And whoever used it knew what he was doing. Familiar with weapons. And who is that?"

"Exactly," Kollberg said. "An army man for example, maybe a butcher."

"A policeman," Gunvald Larsson said.

Of all the men in the department, he was probably the least susceptible to camaraderie and false loyalty.

And that didn't make him particularly popular.

"Come on, Larsson, now you're exaggerating," Kollberg said.

"Could be. Are you going to be working on this?"

Kollberg nodded.

"And you?" he said.

"Looks that way."

They stared at each other without the slightest enthusiasm.

"Maybe we won't have to work together," Kollberg said.

"We can always hope," said Gunvald Larsson.

16.

It was almost ten o'clock in the morning and Martin Beck was sweating in the sunshine as he walked down the quay along Söder Mälarstrand toward Slussen. The sun didn't in fact give out much heat, and the wind from Riddarfjärden was biting cold, but he'd been walking fast and his winter coat was warm.

Hult had offered to drive him to Kungsholmsgatan, but he had turned him down. He was afraid of falling asleep in the car and hoped a brisk walk would wake him up. He unbuttoned his coat and slowed his pace.

When he got to Slussen he went into a telephone booth, called headquarters and was told that Rönn hadn't yet returned. He didn't really have anything to do until Rönn came back, and that would be at least another hour, he thought. If he went straight home, he could be lying in bed in ten minutes. He was really awfully tired, and the thought of his bed was very tempting. If he set the alarm, he could get an hour's sleep.

Martin Beck walked determinedly across Slussplan and into Järntorgsgatan. When he came out into Järntorget he started walking slower. He could imagine how tired he would still be when the alarm went off in an hour, how tough it would be to get up, and how hard to get dressed and on his way to Kungsholm. On the other hand, it would be nice to get out of his clothes for a while and wash or maybe take a shower.

He came to a stop in the middle of the square, as if paralyzed by his own indecision. He could blame it on exhaustion of course, but it irritated him nonetheless.

He changed course and headed toward Skeppsbron. He didn't know what he was going to do when he got there, but when he caught sight of a taxi he made a quick decision. He would go somewhere and have a sauna.

The driver looked to be about Methuselah's age— doddering, toothless and obviously deaf. Martin Beck, who'd gotten into the front seat, hoped that he at least still had his sight. The man was presumably an old taxi owner who hadn't driven his own cab for many years. He took wrong turns incessantly and on one occasion wound up on the left side of the street as if he'd forgotten about the introduction of right-hand traffic. He muttered darkly to himself and his dry old body was periodically shaken by a hacking cough. When he finally brought the car to a halt in front of the Central Baths, Martin Beck gave him much too large a tip in his consternation at having arrived in one piece. He looked at the old man's violently shaking hands and decided not to ask for a receipt.

Martin Beck hesitated for a moment at the ticket window. He usually bathed downstairs where there was a swimming pool, but the thought of a swim didn't appeal to him right now. Instead he bought a ticket to the Turkish section one flight up.

To be on the safe side, he asked the bath attendant who gave him his towels to wake him at eleven o'clock. Then he went into the hottest room and sat there until the sweat ran streaming from his pores. He showered and took a quick dip in the ice-cold water in the tiny pool. Toweled himself dry, wrapped himself in an enormous bath sheet and lay down on the bunk in his cubicle.

He closed his eyes.

He tried to think of something soothing, but his thoughts kept coming back to Harald Hult, sitting there in his desolate impersonal apartment, alone and with nothing to do, wearing his uniform on his day off. A man whose life was filled with one thing—being a policeman. Take that away from him and there'd be nothing left.

Martin Beck wondered what would happen to Hult when he retired. Maybe he would just sit quietly by the window with his hands on the table until he withered away.

Did he even own civilian clothes? Probably not.

His eyes burned and stung beneath their lids, and Martin Beck opened them and stared up at the ceiling. He was too tired to sleep. He put his arm over his face and concentrated on trying to relax. But his muscles stayed taut.

From the massage room came rapid cracking noises and the sound of a bucket of water being dumped on a marble bench. Heavy, rattling snores came from someone in a cubicle nearby.

In his mind's eye, Martin Beck suddenly saw a picture of Nyman's mutilated body. He thought about what Kollberg had told him. About how Nyman had taught him to kill.

Martin Beck had never killed a human being.

He tried to imagine what it would feel like. Not shooting someone—he didn't think that would be hard, maybe because the force it takes to pull a trigger is out of all proportion to the force of the bullet that does the killing. Killing with firearms didn't require any great physical effort, and the distance to the victim ought to make the act feel less immediate. But killing someone directly, with your hands, with a piece of rope, or a knife, or a bayonet, that was another matter. He thought of the body on the marble floor of the hospital, the gaping wound in the throat, the blood, the entrails welling out of the belly, and he knew he'd never be able to kill that way.

During his many years as a policeman, Martin Beck had often asked himself if he was a coward, and the older he got the more certain he was of the answer. Yes, he was a coward. But the question didn't bother him the way it had when he was young.

He didn't know for sure if he was afraid of dying. It was his profession to pry into the way that other people died, and that had blunted his own fear. He rarely thought about his own death.

When the attendant knocked on the wall of the cubicle and announced that it was eleven o'clock, Martin Beck hadn't slept a wink.

17.

He looked at Rönn and felt profoundly guilty. To be sure, they had had about equal amounts of sleep during the last thirty hours, that is to say none at all, but by comparison with his colleague, Martin Beck had passed the time quite pleasantly, in fact to some extent luxuriously.

The whites of Rönn's eyes were by now as red as his nose, while his cheeks and forehead were unwholesomely pale, and the bags beneath his eyes were heavy and dark blue. Yawning uncontrollably, he fumbled his electric razor out of the drawer in his desk.

The tired heroes, thought Martin Beck.

True, he was forty-eight and the elder of the two, but Rönn was forty-three, and the time when they could skip a night's sleep and go unpunished lay irrevocably, and several years, behind them.

On top of it all, Rönn still stubbornly refused to offer information of his own accord, and Martin Beck had to force himself to ask a question.

"Well, what did you find?"

Rönn pointed unhappily at his notebook, as if it had been a dead cat or some other repulsive, shameful thing.

"There," he said thickly. "About twenty names. I only read through the complaints from Nyman's last year as a precinct captain. Then I wrote down the names and addresses of the people who reported him for a couple of years before that. If I'd gone through everything it would have taken all day."

Martin Beck nodded.

"Yes," Rönn went on. "And all day tomorrow too and maybe the next day . . . and the next."

"I wouldn't guess there's any point in digging any deeper than that," said Martin Beck. "I suppose even what you've got there is pretty old."

"Yes, I guess it is," Rönn said.

He picked up his electric razor and left the room at a listless pace, dragging the cord behind him.

Martin Beck sat down at Rönn's desk and with eyebrows knit began to decipher Rönn's cramped and scraggly notations, which always gave him trouble and would probably continue to give him trouble through all eternity.

Afterward he transferred the names, addresses and nature of the complaints to a lined stenographer's tablet.

John Bertilsson, unskilled laborer, Götgatan 20, brutality.

And so forth.

When Rönn came back from the washroom, the list was finished. It included twenty-two names.

Rönn's ablutions had not managed to affect his appearance, which was if possible even more wretched than before, but hopefully he felt a little less shabby. To expect him to feel less exhausted would have been an unreasonable demand.

Maybe some kind of encouragement would be in place. A "pep talk," that's what they called it these days.

"Okay, Einar, I know both of us ought to go home and go to bed. But if we stick with it for a while longer maybe we can come up with something conclusive. It's worth the effort, isn't it?"

"Yes, I guess it is," said Rönn skeptically.

"For example, if you'll take the first ten names and I take the rest, we can pretty quickly locate most of these people and cross them off the list, if nothing else. Okay?"

"Sure. If you say so."

His voice didn't carry an ounce of conviction, which is not even to mention clichés like resolve and fighting spirit.

Rönn blinked his eyes and shivered uncontrollably, but he sat down very nicely at his desk and pulled the telephone toward him.

In his own mind, Martin Beck had to admit that the whole thing seemed pointless.

In the course of his active career, Nyman had of course maltreated hundreds of people. Only a few of them had lodged written complaints and Rönn's brief investigation had uncovered only a few of those.

But many years of experience had taught him that most of his work was in fact pointless, and that even the things that provided results in the long run almost always looked pointless to begin with.

Martin Beck went into the room next door and started to phone, but after only three calls he got sidetracked and ended up sitting passively with his hand on the receiver. He hadn't succeeded in locating any of the people on the list and was now thinking about something entirely different.

After a while he took out his own notebook, shuffled through it and dialed Nyman's home phone. It was the boy who answered.

"Nyman."

The voice sounded earnestly grown-up.

"This is Inspector Beck. We met last night."

"Yes?"

"How's your mother now?"

"Oh, pretty good. She's much better. Doctor Blomberg was here and then she got a couple hours sleep. Now she seems pretty much okay and ..."

The voice trailed off.

"Yes?"

"... and I mean it wasn't entirely unexpected," said the boy uncertainly. "I mean that Papa's gone. He was awful sick. For such a long time too."

"Do you think your mother can come to the phone?"

"Yes, I'm sure she can. She's out in the kitchen. Wait a moment, I'll go tell her."

"Thank you," said Martin Beck.

He heard steps moving away from the phone.

What kind of a husband and father had a man like Nyman been? It had seemed like a happy home. There was nothing to say he couldn't have been a loving and lovable family man.

His son, in any case, had been very close to tears.

"Yes, hello? This is Anna Nyman."

"Inspector Beck. Just one thing I wanted to ask."

"Yes?"

"How many people knew your husband was in the hospital?"

"There weren't very many," she said slowly.

"But he'd been sick for some time, hadn't he?"

"Yes, that's true. But Stig didn't really want people to find out about it. Although . . ."

"Yes?"

"Some people knew, of course."

"Who? Can you say?"

"The family, first of all."

"Which means?"

"The children and I, of course. And Stig has, had, two younger brothers, one in Gothenburg and one in Boden."

Martin Beck nodded to himself. The letters in the hospital room had indeed been written by Nyman's brothers.

"Anyone else?"

"I'm an only child myself. And my parents are dead, so I don't have any close relatives alive. Except for an uncle, but he lives in America and I've never met him."

"What about your friends?"

"We don't have so many. Didn't have, I mean. Gunnar Blomberg who was here last night, we saw a lot of him, and then he was Stig's doctor too. He knew of course."

"I see."

"And then there's Captain Palm and his wife, he was an old friend of my husband's from his regiment. We saw them a good deal."

"Any others?"

"No. There really aren't. We had very few real friends. Only the ones I've named."

She paused. Martin waited.

"Stig used to say . . ."

She left the sentence unfinished.

"Yes, what did he used to say?"

"That a policeman never really has many friends."

That was God's own truth. Martin Beck himself had

no friends. Except for his daughter, and Kollberg. And a woman named Åsa Torell. But she was also on the force.

And then maybe Per Månsson, a policeman in Malmö.

"And these people knew your husband had been admitted to Mount Sabbath?"

"Well, no, I wouldn't say that. The only person who knew exactly where he was was Doctor Blomberg. Of our friends, that is."

"Who visited him?"

"Stefan and I. We went every day."

"No one else?"

"No."

"Not even Doctor Blomberg?"

"No. Stig didn't want anyone to come except me and our son. He didn't really even want Stefan to come."

"Why not?"

"He didn't want anyone to see him. You understand . . ."

Martin Beck waited.

"Well," she said finally. "Stig had always been an unusually strong and vigorous man. Now toward the end he'd grown quite thin and weak and I suppose he was ashamed for people to see him."

"Mmm," said Martin Beck.

"Although Stefan didn't care about that. He worshipped his papa. They were very close."

"What about your daughter?"

"Stig never cared for her the same way. Do you have children yourself?"

"Yes."

"Both boys and girls?"

"Yes."

"Then you know how it is. With fathers and sons, I mean."

As a matter of fact he didn't know. And he thought about it for such a long time that she finally broke in.

"Are you still there, Inspector Beck?"

"Yes, of course. Yes. What about the neighbors?"

"The neighbors?"

"Yes, did they know your husband was in the hospital?"

"Of course not."

"How did you explain the fact that he wasn't at home?"

"I didn't explain it at all. We don't see each other socially."

"What about your son? Maybe he mentioned it to some of his friends?"

"Stefan? No, absolutely not. He knew what his father wanted. It would never occur to him to do anything Stig didn't like. Except that he went with me to visit him every evening. And deep down I think Stig liked that."

Martin Beck made some notes on the steno pad in front of him and then summed it up.

"That means, then, that only you, Stefan, Doctor Blomberg and Inspector Nyman's two brothers knew exactly where your husband was—in which ward and in which room."

"Yes."

"Then that's about all. Just one more thing."

"Yes, what?"

"Which of his colleagues did your husband see outside of work?"

"I don't understand."

Martin Beck put down his pen and massaged the bridge of his nose between his thumb and forefinger. Had he really put the question that badly?

"What I mean is this—what people in the police department did you and your husband see socially?"

"Why, none at all."

"What?"

"What do you mean?"

"Didn't your husband have any friends in the department? People he saw in his off-hours?"

"No. During the twenty-six years Stig and I were married, no policeman ever set foot in our home."

"Do you really mean that?"

"Yes I do. You yourself and that man you had with you last night would be the only ones. But Stig was already dead by then."

"But there must have been messengers, even if they

were only subordinates who came to fetch him or leave things for him."

"Yes, that's right. Orderlies."

"Beg pardon?"

"That's what my husband used to call them, the men who came here. That happened every now and then. But they were never allowed inside the door. Stig was very particular about that."

"Really?"

"Yes. Always. If a patrolman came to pick him up or leave something or something else, we never let him in. If it was I or one of the children who went to the door, we always asked whoever it was to wait and then closed the door until Stig could come."

"Was that his idea?"

"Yes. He told us quite distinctly that that's the way it would be. Once and for all."

"But after all he had colleagues he'd worked with for years and years. Was the same thing true of them?"

"Yes."

"And you don't know any of them?"

"No. At least not more than their names."

"But he used to talk about them at least?"

"Very seldom."

"His superiors then?"

"As I said, very seldom. You see, one of Stig's principles was that his job wasn't to interfere with his private life in any way."

"But you know some of them by name, you said. Which ones?"

"Well, some of the higher officials. The National Chief of Police, and the Commissioner, naturally, and the Superintendent . . ."

"Of the regular metropolitan police?"

"Yes," she said. "Is there more than one superintendent?"

Rönn came into the room with some papers. Martin Beck stared at him blankly. Then he gathered his wits and went on with the conversation.

"But he must have mentioned the names of some of the people he worked with directly."

"Yes, one at least. I know he had a subordinate he

set great store by. A man named Hult. Stig mentioned
him now and then. They'd worked together for a long
time even before we met."

"So you know Hult?"

"No. As far as I know I've never even seen him."

"No?"

"No. But I've talked to him on the telephone."

"Is that all?"

"Can you wait a moment, Mrs. Nyman?"

"Yes, of course."

Martin Beck put the receiver down on the table in
front of him. Thought hard while he rubbed his hairline
with the tips of his fingers. Rönn yawned.

He put the receiver back to his ear.

"Mrs. Nyman?"

"Yes."

"Do you know Captain Hult's first name?"

"Yes, it just happens I do. Palmon Harald Hult. On
the other hand, I didn't know his rank."

"It just happens, you say?"

"Yes, just by chance. I have the name written down
right here in front of me. On the telephone pad. Palmon
Harald Hult."

"Who wrote it there?"

"I did."

Martin Beck didn't say anything.

"Mr. Hult phoned last evening and asked for my husband. He was very upset when he heard Stig was sick."

"And you gave him the address of the hospital?"

"Yes. He wanted to send flowers. And as I said, I
knew who he was. He was the only person I'd think of
giving the address to, except . . ."

"Yes?"

"Well, the National Chief or the Commissioner or the
Superintendent, of course . . ."

"I understand. And so you gave Hult the address?"

"Yes."

She paused.

"What do you mean?" she said then, with dawning
confusion.

"Nothing," Martin Beck said soothingly. "I'm sure it
doesn't mean a thing."

"But you seem so . . ."

"It's just that we have to check out everything, Mrs. Nyman. You've been very helpful. Thank you."

"Thank you," she said bewilderedly.

"Thank you," Martin Beck repeated, and hung up.

Rönn was leaning against the doorjamb.

"I think I've checked as far as I can for now," he said. "Two of them are dead. And no one knows a thing about this damned Eriksson."

"Uh-hunh," said Martin Beck absently, and printed a name on the steno pad.

PALMON HARALD HULT.

18.

If Hult was at work, then he ought to be at his desk. He was getting on in years and no longer did anything but paperwork, at least officially.

But the man who answered at Maria police station seemed utterly uncomprehending.

"Hult? No, he's not here. He always has Saturdays and Sundays off."

"Hasn't he been in at all today?"

"No."

"Are you sure?"

"Yeah. Anyway I haven't seen him."

"Would you mind asking the others?"

"What others?"

"I hope we're not so understaffed there's only one man in the whole Second Precinct," said Martin Beck, a little irritated. "You're not at the station all alone, are you?"

"No, of course not," the man said, somewhat dampened. "Wait a minute. I'll ask."

Martin Beck heard the clatter of the receiver on the table and the sound of footsteps clumping off.

And a distant voice.

"Hey everybody," it shouted, "has anyone seen Hult

today? That snob Beck from Homicide's on the phone and . . ."

The rest of it was lost in noise and other voices.

Martin Beck waited, throwing a weary glance at Rönn, who looked even more wearily at his wristwatch.

Why did the man at Maria think he was a snob? Presumably because he didn't call people by their first names. Martin Beck had a hard time using first names to patrolmen who were hardly dry behind the ears, and he couldn't get used to their calling him "Martin."

And yet he was certainly no stickler for formality.

How had a man like Nyman reacted in such situations?

There was a clattering in the receiver.

"Yes, about Hult . . ."

"Yes?"

"As a matter of fact he was here for a while. About an hour and a half ago. But apparently he left again almost right away."

"Where to?"

"Nobody knows."

Martin Beck let this generalization pass without objection.

"Thanks," he said.

Just to be sure, he dialed Hult's home phone, but as he'd expected there was no answer, and he hung up after the fifth ring.

"Who are you looking for?" Rönn asked.

"Hult."

"Oh."

You couldn't say Rönn was especially observant, thought Martin Beck irritably.

"Einar?" he said.

"Yeah?"

"Hult called Nyman's wife last night and got the address of the hospital."

"Oh?"

"We might ask ourselves why."

"He probably wanted to send flowers or something," said Rönn disinterestedly. "Hult and Nyman were buddies, after all."

"Apparently there weren't very many people who knew Nyman was at Mount Sabbath."

"So that's why Hult had to call up and ask," Rönn said.

"Curious coincidence."

This was not a question, and Rönn quite correctly neglected to answer it. Instead he changed the subject.

"Oh yes, I told you I couldn't get hold of this man Eriksson."

"Which man Eriksson?"

"Åke Eriksson. That patrolman who was always writing complaints."

Martin Beck nodded. He remembered the name, although it must have been a long time since it was mentioned much. But it wasn't a name he wanted to remember, and on top of that he was busy thinking about Hult.

He had talked to Hult less than two hours ago. How had he behaved? News of Nyman's murder hadn't produced any reaction at all at first. And then Hult had gone to work, as he'd put it.

Martin Beck hadn't found anything odd in all of that. Hult was a thick-skinned old policeman and fairly slow-witted, anything but impulsive. That he voluntarily lent a hand when a colleague had been killed seemed perfectly natural. In certain situations, Martin Beck would have behaved exactly the same way.

What did seem odd was the telephone call. Why hadn't he said he'd been in touch with Nyman's wife as recently as the evening before? And if his only reason was to send a greeting, why had he called at night?

If, on the other hand, he'd wanted to know Nyman's exact whereabouts for some reason other than sending flowers.

Martin Beck forced himself to interrupt that line of thought.

Had Hult really called at night?

In that case, what time?

He needed more information.

Martin Beck sighed heavily, lifted the receiver and, for the third time, dialed Anna Nyman's number.

This time it was she herself who answered.

"Oh yes," she said resignedly. "Inspector Beck."

"I'm sorry, but I have to ask you a few more questions about that telephone call."

"Yes?"

"You said that Captain Hult called you last night?"

"Yes?"

"What time?"

"Fairly late, but I can't say exactly when."

"Well about what time?"

"Well . . ."

"Had you already gone to bed?"

"Oh no . . . no, wait a moment."

She put down the phone and Martin Beck drummed his fingers impatiently on the table. He could hear her talking to someone, probably her son, but he couldn't distinguish the words.

"Yes, hello?"

"Yes."

"I was talking to Stefan. We were sitting watching television. First a movie with Humphrey Bogart, but it was so unpleasant we switched to Channel Two. There was a variety show with Benny Hill and it had just started when the phone rang."

"Splendid. How long had the program been going?"

"Only a few minutes. Five at the most."

"Thank you, Mrs. Nyman. There's just one more thing."

"Yes, what?"

"Can you remember exactly what Hult said?"

"No, not word for word. He just asked to speak to Stig and so I said——"

"Forgive me for interrupting. Did he say, 'Can I talk to Stig?' "

"No, of course not. He was quite correct."

"How so?"

"He apologized and asked if he might speak to Inspector Nyman."

"Why did he apologize?"

"For calling so late, of course."

"And what did you say?"

"I asked who was calling. Or to be exact, I said, 'May I say who's calling?' "

"And what did Mr. Hult say then?"

" 'I'm a colleague of Inspector Nyman's.' Something like that. And then he said his name."

"And what did you say?"

"As I told you before, I recognized the name immediately and I knew he'd called before and that he was one of the few people Stig really thought well of."

"Called before, you say. How often?"

"A few times over the years. When my husband was well and at home, he was almost always the one who answered the phone, so this Mr. Hult may have called any number of times."

"And what did you say then?"

"I told you all this before."

"I'm sorry if I seem persistent," said Martin Beck. "But this could be important."

"I said Stig was ill. And he seemed surprised and sorry and asked me if it was serious and . . ."

"And?"

"And I said I was afraid it was quite serious and that Stig was in the hospital. And then he asked if he might go visit him, and I said my husband would probably rather he didn't."

"Did that seem to satisfy him?"

"Yes of course. Harald Hult knew Stig very well. From work."

"But he said he was going to send flowers?"

Leading question, he thought to himself. Damn.

"Yes. And he wanted to write a note. So I said Stig was at Mount Sabbath and I gave him the room number and the ward. I remember Stig's saying a couple of times that Hult was dependable and correct."

"And then?"

"He begged my pardon again. Thanked me and said good night."

Martin Beck thanked her too, and in his haste very nearly said good night himself. Then he turned to Rönn.

"Did you watch TV last night?"

Rönn responded with an injured look.

"No, of course not. You were on duty. But can you find out what time the program with Benny Hill started on Channel Two?"

"I guess I can," Rönn said, and slouched out to the day room.

He came back with a newspaper in his hand, studied it for a long time.

"Nine twenty-five."

"So Hult called at nine thirty in the evening. That's pretty late unless he had some fairly pressing business."

"Didn't he then?"

"He doesn't seem to have mentioned it, in any case. On the other hand he was careful to find out where Nyman was."

"Sure. Because he was going to send flowers."

Martin Beck looked at Rönn for a long time. He needed a chance to talk this thing through.

"Einar, can you listen for a while?"

"Yes, I guess I can."

Martin Beck summarized everything he knew about Hult's actions during the preceding twenty-four hours, from the telephone call to the conversation on Reimersholme and the fact that, at the moment, the man couldn't be located.

"Do you think it was Hult who knifed Nyman?"

The question was unusually direct to have come from Rönn.

"Well, no. I guess I wouldn't say that exactly."

"I think it sounds pretty farfetched," Rönn said. "And pretty peculiar."

"Hult's behavior is pretty peculiar too, to put it mildly."

Rönn didn't respond.

"In any case, I want to get hold of Hult and ask him some questions about this telephone call," said Martin Beck energetically.

The firmness in his tone made no great impression on Rönn, who yawned widely.

"Send out a call on the radio then," he said. "He can't be far away."

Martin Beck looked at him in surprise.

"Yes, that's really a pretty constructive suggestion."

"What do you mean 'constructive'?" Rönn said, as if he'd been accused of something unsavory.

Martin Beck picked up the phone again and started

giving instructions to the effect that Captain Harald Hult should be requested to contact the Violence Squad on Kungsholmsgatan as soon as he could be located.

Finished with that, he sat at his desk with his head in his hands.

There was something that didn't fit. And still that feeling of danger. From whom? Hult? Or was there something else he'd overlooked?

"Though there is one thing," Rönn said.

"What?"

"Well, if I called your wife and asked for you——" He interrupted himself.

"No, that wouldn't happen," he muttered. "You're divorced."

"What were you going to say?"

"Nothing," said Rönn unhappily. "I wasn't thinking. I don't want to mess in your private life."

"But what were you going to say?"

Rönn thought out a better way of putting it.

"Well, if you were married and I called and got your wife and asked to speak to you and she asked me who I was, well . . ."

"Well what?"

"Well, I wouldn't say, 'This is Einar Valentino Rönn.' "

"Who in the world is that?"

"Me. That's my name. After some movie star. My mother was a little weird sometimes."

Martin Beck perked up immediately.

"So you mean . . . ?"

"I mean it seems sort of odd and unlikely that Hult calls up Nyman's wife and says this is Palmon Harald Hult."

"How did you know what his name was?"

"You've got it printed on Melander's tablet there. And what's more . . ."

"What's more what?"

"What's more, I've got it in my own papers. On Åke Eriksson's J.O. petition."

Martin Beck's gaze slowly cleared.

"Good, Einar," he said. "Very good."

Rönn yawned.

"Who's on duty here?" Martin Beck asked suddenly.

"Gunvald. But he's not here. He's hopeless about things like that."

"There must be somebody else."

"Yes. Strömgren."

"And where's Melander?"

"Home, I suppose. He's got Saturdays off these days."

"I think maybe we'll take a closer look at friend Eriksson," said Martin Beck. "The trouble is, I don't remember any details."

"Me neither," Rönn said. "But Melander remembers. He remembers everything."

"Tell Strömgren to pull out everything he can find on Åke Eriksson. And call Melander and ask him to come down here. Right away."

"That may not be so easy. He's an assistant chief inspector now. He doesn't like to give up his free time."

"Use my name," said Martin Beck.

"Yes, I guess I will," Rönn said, and left the room with dragging steps.

Two minutes later he was back.

"Strömgren's looking," he said.

"And Melander?"

"He's on his way, but . . ."

"But what?"

"He didn't sound happy about it."

Well, that would be asking the impossible.

Martin Beck waited. First of all for Hult to turn up.

And then for the chance to talk to Fredrik Melander.

Fredrik Melander was one of the Violence Squad's few priceless resources. He was the man with the legendary memory. An awful bore, but a detective with unusual qualities. The whole of modern technology seemed paltry by comparison, for in the course of a few minutes Melander could sort out everything of importance he'd ever heard, seen or read about some particular person or some particular subject and then present it clearly and lucidly in narrative form.

There wasn't a computer in the world that could do the same.

On the other hand, he wasn't much with a pen. Martin Beck studied some notes on Melander's pad. They were written in a cramped, distinctive hand that was guaranteed to be illegible.

19.

Rönn leaned against the doorjamb and giggled. Martin Beck looked at him wonderingly.

"What are you laughing at?"

"Well, it just struck me that you're looking for a policeman and I'm looking for a policeman and it may be the same man."

"The same man?"

"No, I guess that couldn't be," Rönn said. "Åke Eriksson is Åke Eriksson and Palmon Harald Hult is Palmon Harald Hult."

Martin Beck wondered if maybe he shouldn't send Rönn home. There was some question as to whether Rönn's presence was even legal, since according to a new law that had gone into effect at the beginning of the year, no policeman was allowed to serve more than a hundred and fifty hours of overtime per year, nor more than fifty in any given quarter. Theoretically, this could mean that a policeman drew his salary but was at the same time forbidden to work. There was one exception —situations of extreme urgency.

Was this one of those? Conceivably.

Or maybe he ought to put Rönn under arrest. The quarter was only four days old, and Rönn had already used up his overtime quota. It would undeniably be a first in the history of detection.

Otherwise the work was going along normally. To the extent that Strömgren had searched out a mass of old papers and periodically came in with more.

Martin Beck regarded them with growing distaste.

He kept thinking of more questions he ought to ask Anna Nyman.

But with his hand on the phone, he hesitated. Wasn't it a little much to call her again so soon? Couldn't he get Rönn to do it? In that case he'd have to call her anyway and apologize not only for himself but also for Rönn.

In the face of that dismal prospect he recovered his courage, lifted the receiver and dialed the number to the bereaved household for the fourth time.

"Nymans'. Hello?"

The widow's voice sounded more spirited every time he heard it. Everything was on its way back to normal. One more demonstration of that resilience for which the human race was so well known. He pulled himself together.

"Hello, this is Beck again."

"But it's only ten minutes since I talked to you . . ."

"I know. I'm sorry. I suppose it's painful for you to talk about this . . . incident."

Couldn't he really have found a better word?

"I'm beginning to get used to it," she said with a certain chill. "What would you like now, Chief Inspector?"

In any case she certainly knew her ranks.

"Well, I'd like to go back to that phone call."

"From Captain Hult?"

"Yes, right. You said that wasn't the first time you'd spoken to him."

"No."

"Did you recognize his voice?"

"Of course not."

"Why 'of course'?"

"Because then I wouldn't have had to ask who it was."

Mother! Well that's the way it goes. He should have let Rönn make the call after all.

"Didn't you think of that, Inspector?" she asked.

"No, as a matter of fact I didn't."

Most people would have blushed or hemmed and hawed. Not Martin Beck. He went on undaunted.

"So it could have been anyone at all?"

"Doesn't it seem odd that just anyone at all would call up and say his name was Palmon Harald Hult?"

"I mean it could have been someone other than Hult."

"Who?"

Good question, he thought.

"Could you tell if it was an older or a younger man?"

"No."

"Can you describe the voice at all?"

"Well . . . it was distinct. Maybe a little gruff."

Yes, that was an excellent description of Hult's voice. Gruff and distinct. But there were a lot of policemen who talked that way, particularly the ones with a military background. And not only policemen of course.

"Wouldn't it be easier to ask Captain Hult?" the woman said.

Martin Beck declined to comment. Instead he headed into deeper water.

"Being a policeman almost always involves making a few enemies."

"Yes, you said so before. The second time we talked. Are you aware, Inspector, that this is our fifth conversation in less than twelve hours?"

"I'm sorry. You said you didn't know your husband had any enemies."

"That's right."

"But of course you knew he had certain professional problems."

It sounded as if she had laughed.

"Now I really don't understand what you mean."

Yes, she had actually laughed.

"What I mean," said Martin Beck mercilessly, "is that many people seemed to think your husband was a bad policeman and outright derelict in his duty."

That hit home. Gravity was restored.

"Are you joking, Inspector?"

"No," he said, a little more gently. "I'm not joking. Your husband incurred a lot of complaints."

"For what?"

"Brutality."

She drew a sharp breath.

"That's utterly absurd," she said. "You must be confusing him with someone else."

"I don't believe so."

"But Stig was the gentlest person I ever met. For example, we've always had a dog. Dogs, I mean. Four of them, one after the other. Stig loved them, and he was endlessly patient, even before they were housebroken. He'd work with them for weeks without losing his temper."

"Really?"

"And he never so much as lifted his hand to the children, especially when they were little."

Martin Beck had often raised his hand to his children, especially when they were little.

"So he never said anything about his troubles on the job."

"No. I've already told you he practically never mentioned his job. What's more, I don't believe that talk for a moment. There simply must be some mistake."

"But he must have had certain opinions? In general I mean?"

"Yes, he thought society was suffering a moral breakdown. Because of the government."

Well, that was a view you could hardly blame him for. The trouble was that Stig Nyman belonged to a little minority that would undoubtedly make everything even worse if they got the chance.

"Was there anything else?" Mrs. Nyman asked. "I really have a great deal to do."

"No, not right now anyway. I'm very sorry I've had to trouble you."

"It's quite all right."

She didn't sound convinced.

"The only thing might be if we have to ask you to identify the voice."

"Captain Hult's?"

"Yes, do you think you'd recognize it now?"

"Very likely. Good-bye."

"Good-bye."

Martin Beck pushed away the telephone. Strömgren came in with still more papers. Rönn stood by the window looking out, his glasses pushed down to the tip of his nose.

"Yes indeed," he said tranquilly.

Another quarter heard from.

"What branch of the service was Hult in?"

"The cavalry," Rönn said.

A bully's paradise.

"And Eriksson?"

"He was in the artillery."

There was silence for fifteen seconds.

"Is it the bayonet you're thinking of?" Rönn said at last.

"Yes."

"Yes, I thought so."

"What do you mean?"

"It's just that anyone can buy one of those things for five crowns. From army surplus."

Martin Beck said nothing.

He'd never been awfully impressed with Rönn, but it had never occurred to him that the feeling might be mutual.

There was a tapping on the door.

Melander.

Probably the only man in the world who would tap on his own door.

20.

Lennart Kollberg was uneasy about the time factor. He had a feeling something dramatic ought to happen, but so far nothing had interrupted the routine. The body was gone and the floor had been washed. The bloody bedclothes had been removed. The bed had been rolled away in one direction and the night table in another. All the personal belongings had been put in plastic bags, which had then been placed in a sack. This now lay in the corridor waiting for someone to collect it. The lab men were gone and not even a chalk outline on the floor recalled the existence of the late Stig Nyman. That method was old-fashioned and rarely used any more. The only ones who missed it seemed to be the newspaper photographers.

As a matter of fact the only thing left in the room

was the visitor's chair, and Kollberg sat on that himself, and thought.

What does a person do after killing someone? He knew from experience that there were a lot of answers to that question.

Kollberg had killed a man himself one time. What had he done afterward? He'd thought about it long and hard, for years in fact, and in the end he'd turned in his service revolver, with the license and everything, and said he never wanted to carry arms again. That had all happened several years ago and he had a vague memory that the last time he'd carried a pistol was in Motala in the summer of 1964, during the notorious Roseanna case. But he still sometimes caught himself thinking of that unhappy occasion. Like when he looked at himself in the mirror. That person there has killed a man.

During his years on the force he'd stood face to face with more murderers than he cared to think about. And he was aware of the fact that a person's behavior after committing a violent act has infinite variations. Some people throw up, some people eat a hearty meal, and some people kill themselves. Others panic and run, to no place in particular, just run, and still others quite simply go home and go to bed.

Trying to make guesses on that point was not only difficult, it was also professionally unsound, since it could lead the investigation down the wrong track.

Nevertheless, there was something about the circumstances surrounding Nyman's murder that made him ask himself what the man with the bayonet had done afterward, and what he was doing right now.

What circumstances? In part the purely external violence, which must be an expression of an inner violence at least as great and thus destined to further expression.

But was it really that simple? Kollberg remembered the way he'd felt when Nyman was teaching him to be a paratrooper. At first he'd felt weak and sick and couldn't eat, but it wasn't long before he'd climb out of his pile of steaming offal, throw off his protective clothes, shower and head straight for the canteen. And wolf down coffee and pastry. So even things like that could get to be routine.

Another circumstance that influenced Kollberg's thinking was the way Martin Beck had acted. Kollberg was a very sensitive man, not least of all in regard to his boss. He knew Martin Beck inside and out and had no trouble picking up the nuances in his behavior. Today Martin Beck had seemed uneasy, maybe downright frightened, and that was a thing that happened rarely and never without cause.

So now he sat here with his question. What had the murderer done after the murder?

Gunvald Larsson, never reluctant to guess and take chances, had had an immediate answer.

"He probably went straight home and shot himself," he'd said.

It was doubtless a possibility worth considering. And maybe it was as simple as that. Gunvald Larsson was often right, but it happened at least as often that he guessed wrong.

Kollberg was prepared to admit that that was only human, but absolutely nothing more. He had always considered Gunvald Larsson's qualifications as a policeman highly doubtful.

And it was just this dubious person who now interrupted Kollberg's speculations by marching into the room together with a corpulent bald-headed man in his sixties. The man looked frustrated, but most people did in the company of Gunvald Larsson.

"This is Lennart Kollberg," Gunvald Larsson said.

Kollberg stood up and looked questioningly at the stranger, and Gunvald Larsson completed his laconic introduction.

"This is Nyman's medico."

They shook hands.

"Kollberg."

"Blomberg."

And Gunvald Larsson started throwing out meaningless questions.

"What's your first name?"

"Carl-Axel."

"How long have you been Nyman's doctor?"

"Over twenty years."

"What was he suffering from?"

"Well, it may be a little involved for a layman . . ."

"Go right ahead."

"It's actually pretty complicated even for a doctor."

"Oh?"

"The fact is I've just come from looking at the X rays. Seventy of them."

"And?"

"The diagnosis is largely positive. Good news."

"What?"

Gunvald Larsson was so taken aback he looked almost dangerous, and the doctor hurriedly went on.

"Well, I mean if he were still alive, of course. Very good news."

"Which is to say?"

"That he could have been cured."

Blomberg thought for a moment and then modified his statement.

"Well, at least restored to relative good health."

"What was wrong with him?"

"As I said, we've now determined that. Stig had a medium-sized cyst on the jejunum."

"On the what?"

"The small intestine. And a small tumor in the liver."

"And what does that mean?"

"That he could have been restored to a state of relative good health, as I said. The cyst was operable. It could have been removed. It was not of a malignant nature."

"What's 'malignant'?"

"Cancer. It kills you."

Gunvald Larsson seemed noticeably encouraged.

"That isn't so hard to understand," he said.

"As you gentlemen may know, however, we cannot operate on the liver. But the tumor was very small, and Stig ought to have been able to live for several more years."

Doctor Blomberg nodded in affirmation of himself.

"Stig is physically strong. His general condition is excellent."

"What?"

"Was, I mean. Good blood pressure and a strong heart. Excellent general condition."

Gunvald Larsson seemed to have had enough.

The physician made motions as if to go.

"One moment, Doctor," Kollberg said.

"Yes?"

"You were Inspector Nyman's doctor for a long time and knew him well?"

"Yes, that's right."

"What kind of a person was Nyman?"

"Yes, aside from his general condition," said Gunvald Larsson.

"I'm not a psychiatrist," said Blomberg and shook his head. "I prefer to stick to internal medicine."

But Kollberg wasn't ready to give up quite yet.

"Still you must have had some opinion about him."

"Stig Nyman was a complex human being, as we all are," said the doctor cryptically.

"Is that all you have to say?"

"Yes."

"Thank you."

"Good-bye," said Gunvald Larsson.

And there the interview ended.

When the internist had gone, Gunvald Larsson turned to one of his more irritating habits. He pulled systematically at each of his long fingers, one after the other, until the knuckles cracked. In several cases he had to pull two or three times. This was particularly true of his right index finger, which didn't crack until the eighth attempt.

Kollberg followed the procedure with resigned aversion.

"Larsson?" he said at last.

"Yes, what?"

"Why do you do that?"

"That's my business," said Gunvald Larsson.

Kollberg went on trying to guess riddles.

"Larsson," he said after a while, "can you think yourself into the position of this man who killed Nyman, and the way he reasoned? Afterward?"

"How do you know it was a man?"

"Very few women know how to handle that kind of a weapon, and still fewer wear a size twelve shoe. Well, can you? Think yourself into his situation?"

Gunvald Larsson looked at him with steady clear-blue eyes.

"No, I can't. How the hell could I?"

He lifted his head, brushed the blond hair out of his eyes, and listened.

"What the hell's all that noise?" he said.

Shouts and excited voices could be heard somewhere nearby. Kollberg and Gunvald Larsson immediately left the room and went outside. One of the police department's black and white VW busses stood by the foot of the steps, and about fifty feet farther off there were five young patrolmen and an older uniformed police officer in the process of pushing back a crowd of civilians.

The patrolmen had linked hands and their commander was waving his rubber nightstick threateningly above his gray crew cut.

Among the crowd were some press photographers, a few female hospital orderlies in white coats, a cabdriver in his uniform, and a number of other people of various ages. The usual collection of thrill-seekers. Several of them were protesting loudly, and one of the younger ones picked up an object from the ground. An empty beer can. He threw it at the policemen and missed.

"Get 'em, boys," the officer yelled. "That'll be enough of that."

More white nightsticks came into sight.

"Hold it!" demanded Gunvald Larsson in a stentorian bellow.

All activity ceased.

Gunvald Larsson walked toward the crowd.

"What's this all about?"

"I'm clearing the area in front of the cordon," said the older policeman.

The gold stripe on his sleeve indicated that he was a captain.

"But there's nothing here to cordon off, for Christ's sake," said Gunvald Larsson angrily.

"No, Hult, that's true enough," Kollberg said. "And where did you get these fellows?"

"An emergency squad from the Fifth Precinct," said the man, coming automatically to attention. "They were here already and I assumed command."

"Well stop this nonsense at once," said Gunvald Larsson. "Put a guard on the steps to keep unauthorized people out of the building itself. I doubt even that's really necessary. And send the rest of them back to the precinct station. I'm sure they need them more back there."

From inside the police bus came the sound of short-wave static and then a metallic voice.

"Captain Harald Hult is requested to contact central and report to Chief Inspector Beck."

Hult still had his nightstick in his hand and looked sullenly at the two detectives.

"Well," said Kollberg. "Aren't you going to contact central? It sounds like someone's looking for you."

"All in good time," the man said. "Anyway I'm here voluntarily."

"I don't think we need any volunteers here," said Kollberg.

He was wrong.

"What a lot of bullshit," said Gunvald Larsson. "But at least I've done my bit around here."

He was also wrong.

Just as he took the first long stride toward his car, a shot rang out and a shrill, frantic voice started calling for help.

Gunvald Larsson stopped in bewilderment and looked at his watch. It was ten minutes after twelve.

Kollberg also responded at once.

Maybe this was what he'd been waiting for.

21.

"As to Eriksson," Melander said, putting down the bundle of papers, "it's a long story. You must know some of it already."

"Assume we don't know anything and tell it to us from the beginning," said Martin Beck.

Melander leaned back in his chair and started to fill his pipe.

"Okay," he said. "From the beginning then. Åke Eriksson was born in Stockholm in 1935. He was an only child, and his father was a lathe operator. He left high school in '54, did his national service the following year, and when he got out he applied to the police force. He started OCS night school and the Police Academy at the same time."

He lit his pipe elaborately and blew small clouds of smoke across the tabletop. Rönn, who was sitting across from him, reproached him with an ostentatious cough. Melander took no notice and went on puffing.

"Okay," he said, "that's a short résumé of the earlier and comparatively less interesting half of Eriksson's life. In 1956 he started as a patrolman in Katarina precinct. There's not much to be said about the next few years. As far as I can understand, he was a pretty average policeman, neither awfully good nor awfully bad. There were no complaints about him, but on the other hand I can't recall that he distinguished himself in any way."

"Was he in Katarina that whole time?" asked Martin Beck, who was standing by the door with one arm on the filing cabinet.

"No," Melander said. "He was stationed in probably three or four different precincts those first four years."

He stopped and furrowed his brow. Then he took his pipe out of his mouth and pointed the stem at Martin Beck.

"Correction," he said. "I said he didn't distinguish himself in any way. That's wrong. He was an excellent shot, always placed very high in the matches."

"Yes," Rönn said. "I remember that myself. He was good with a pistol."

"He was excellent at long range too," Melander said. "And all this time he went on with his voluntary officer's training. He used to spend his vacations at OCS camps."

"You said he was in three or four different precincts those first years," said Martin Beck. "Was he ever in Stig Nyman's precinct?"

"He was for a while, yes. Fall of '57 and all of '58. Then Nyman got a new precinct."

"Do you know anything about the way Nyman treated Eriksson? He could be pretty rough on the ones he didn't like."

"There's nothing to indicate he was harder on Eriksson than on the other young men. And Eriksson's complaints against Nyman don't have much to do with that period. But knowing something about Nyman's methods for 'making men out of mama's boys,' as he used to put it. I think we can assume that Åke Eriksson got his share."

Melander had directed most of his remarks to Martin Beck. Now he looked at Rönn, who sat crumpled in the visitor's chair and looked as if he might fall asleep at any moment. Martin Beck followed his glance.

"A cup of coffee doesn't sound like such a bad idea, does it, Einar?" he said.

Rönn straightened up.

"No, I guess not," he mumbled. "I'll get it."

He shambled out of the room and Martin Beck watched him and wondered if he looked that miserable himself.

When Rönn had come back with the coffee and collapsed in his easy chair again, Martin Beck looked at Melander.

"Go on, Fredrik," he said.

Melander put down his pipe and slurped his coffee thoughtfully.

"Jesus," he said. "That's awful."

He pushed away the plastic mug and went back to his beloved pipe.

"Well, at the beginning of 1959, Åke Eriksson got married. The girl was five years younger than he, and her name was Marja. She was Finnish, but she'd lived in Sweden for several years and had a job as an assistant in a photographic studio. Her Swedish wasn't very good, which may have something to do with what happened later. They had a baby in December the same year they were married, and she then quit her job and became a housewife. When the child was a year and a half old, that is, in the summer of '61, Marja Eriksson died under circumstances you can hardly have forgotten."

Rönn nodded in sad assent. Or was it simply that he was about to doze off?

"No, but don't worry about that," said Martin Beck. "Tell us anyway."

"Well," said Melander, "this may be where Stig Nyman comes into the story. And Harald Hult, who at that time was a sergeant in Nyman's precinct. Marja Eriksson died at their precinct station. In a drunk cell, the night between the twenty-sixth and twenty-seventh of June, 1961."

"Were Nyman and Hult at the station that night?" asked Martin Beck.

"Nyman was there when they brought her in, but he went home later on, at some hour that hasn't been determined exactly. Hult was out on patrol that night, but it's quite certain that he happened to be at the station when she was discovered dead."

Melander straightened out a paper clip and started to clean out his pipe into the ashtray.

"There was an investigation eventually, and the chain of events was reconstructed. What happened seems to have been the following. During the day on June twenty-sixth, Marja Eriksson and her daughter went out to visit a friend of hers in Vaxholm. The photographer she'd worked for previously had asked her to help him with a two-week assignment, and Marja's girl friend was going to take care of the child. Late in the afternoon she went back into town again. Åke Eriksson finished work at seven that evening, and she wanted to be home ahead of him. It's worth noting that Eriksson was not assigned to Nyman's precinct at that time."

Martin Beck's legs were starting to get tired. Since the only two chairs in the room were taken, he left the filing cabinet and walked over to the window and half sat against the sill. He nodded to Melander to go on.

"Marja Eriksson had diabetes and needed regular injections of insulin. There weren't many people who knew about that—the girl friend in Vaxholm, for example, did not. Marja Eriksson never used to be careless about her injections—for that matter she wasn't in a position where she could afford to be careless—but on that particular day, for some reason, she'd left her syringe at home."

Both Martin Beck and Rönn now looked at Melander intently, as if they meant to weigh his version of the story very carefully.

"Two patrolmen from Nyman's precinct discovered Marja Eriksson just after seven o'clock in the evening. She was sitting on a bench, and looked to be on her last legs. They tried to talk to her and became convinced that she was under the influence of narcotics, or maybe just blind drunk. They dragged her to a taxi and drove her to the police station. They said themselves at the hearing that they didn't quite know what to do with her when they got her there, since she was virtually helpless. The cabdriver said later that she had said something in a foreign language, that is, Finnish, and it's possible there was some sort of a ruckus in the taxi. The two patrolmen denied it, of course."

Melander paused a long while as he fussed ceremoniously with his pipe.

"Now then, according to what these patrolmen first said, Nyman had a look at her and told them to put her in a drunk cell for the time being. Nyman denied ever having seen the woman, and at a later hearing the patrolmen changed their story and said they guessed Nyman must have been busy with something else when they brought her in. They themselves had been forced to leave again immediately on some urgent mission. According to the cell guard, it was the patrolmen themselves who decided to lock her up. That is to say, everyone blamed everyone else. There wasn't a sound from her cell, and the guard thought she was asleep. There hadn't been any chance of getting a transport to Criminal for nearly three hours. When his relief came, the night guard unlocked the cell and found she was dead. Hult was at the station right then, and he called an ambulance but couldn't get them to take her to the hospital because she was already dead."

"What time did she die?" asked Martin Beck.

"She appeared to have died about an hour earlier."

Rönn straightened up in his chair.

"When you've got diabetes," he said, "I mean, don't people with diseases like that carry a card or something that says what it is that's wrong with them . . ."

"Yes indeed," Melander said. "And Marja Eriksson had one, too—in her purse. But as you probably know, part of the whole problem was that she was never searched. They didn't have any female personnel at the precinct, so she would have been searched here at Criminal. If she'd ever arrived."

Martin Beck nodded.

"Later, at the hearing, Nyman said he'd never seen either the woman or her purse, so the two patrolmen and the guard had to take the whole responsibility. As far as I know, they got off with a warning."

"How did Åke Eriksson react when he found out what had happened?" asked Martin Beck.

"He fell apart and had to go on sick leave for a couple of months. Lost all interest in everything, apparently. When his wife didn't come home, he finally discovered she hadn't taken her syringe. First he called around to all the hospitals and then took his car and went out looking for her, so it was quite some time before he found out she was dead. I don't think they told him the truth right away, but eventually he must have found out what had happened, because in September he sent in his first written complaint against Nyman and Hult. But by then the investigation was already closed."

22.

Melander's office grew quiet.

Melander had clasped his hands behind his neck and was staring at the ceiling, Martin Beck was leaning against the windowsill looking pensively and expectantly at Melander, and Rönn was just sitting.

Finally Martin Beck broke the silence.

"What happened to Eriksson after his wife's death? I mean, not the external events, but what happened to him psychologically?"

"Well, I'm no psychiatrist," Melander said, "and there's no expert opinion, because as far as I know he never went to a doctor after going back to work in September '61. Which he maybe should have done."

"But he was different afterward, wasn't he?"

"Yes," Melander said. "It's obvious he underwent some sort of personality change."

He put his hand on the bundle of papers that Strömgren had gathered from various files.

"Have you read through this?" he asked.

Rönn shook his head.

"Only part of it," said Martin Beck. "That can wait. I think we can get a clear picture faster if you'll summarize it for us."

He thought of adding a word of praise, but didn't, since he knew Melander was immune to flattery.

Melander nodded and put his pipe between his teeth.

"Okay," he said. "When Åke Eriksson went back to work again, he was uncommunicative and quiet and kept to himself as much as possible. The other fellows on his watch tried to cheer him up, but without success. To begin with they were patient with him. They knew what had happened, after all, and they felt sorry for him. But since he never said a word unless it was absolutely necessary, and since he never listened to anyone else either, they all finally tried to avoid having to work with him. He'd been popular before, and they probably hoped he'd be his old self again when the worst of his grief was over. Instead he only got worse—touchy, sullen and downright priggish in his work. He started sending letters full of complaints and threats and accusations, and that went on periodically for years. We've all gotten one or more, I suppose."

"Not me," Rönn said.

"Maybe you haven't gotten any personally, but you've seen his letters to the Violence Squad."

"Yes," Rönn said.

"He started out by reporting Nyman and Hult to the J.O. for breach of duty. He sent in that complaint several times. Then he started reporting everyone in sight for breach of duty, even the governor. He's reported me, and you too, Martin, hasn't he?"

"Oh yes," said Martin Beck. "For not opening an investigation into the murder of his wife. But that was a long time ago, and as a matter of fact I'd forgotten about him."

"By about a year after his wife's death, he'd made himself so impossible that the chief in his precinct asked to have him transferred."

"Do you know what he stated as cause?" Martin Beck asked.

"That inspector was a decent man and apparently he'd closed his eyes to a great deal in Eriksson's case. But in the end it just got to be too much, for the sake of the other men. He said that Eriksson spread disharmony around him, that he was difficult to work with, and that it would be better for Eriksson himself if he were transferred to a precinct where he might feel more at home. That's more or less the way he put it. Anyway, Eriksson was transferred to a new precinct in the summer of '62. He wasn't especially popular there either, and his new chief didn't back him up the way the other one had. The other patrolmen complained about him and he picked up a few demerits."

"What for?" asked Martin Beck. "Was he violent?"

"No, not at all. He was never brutal or anything, rather overly nice, a lot of people thought. He behaved correctly toward everyone he came in contact with. No, apparently the trouble was his ridiculous pedantry. He'd spend hours on things that shouldn't really have taken more than fifteen minutes. He'd submerge himself in unimportant details, and occasionally he'd ignore specific instructions in order to do something completely different that he thought was more important. He overstepped his authority by getting involved in things other people had been assigned to deal with. He criticized both his colleagues and his superiors, in fact that's what all his complaints and reports were about—the way people on the force neglected their jobs, from the cadets in his own precinct all the way up to the Chief of Police. I don't doubt he made complaints about the Minister of the Interior, since he was the ultimate chief of police in those days."

"Did he think he was perfect himself?" Rönn said. "Maybe he had delusions of grandeur."

"Like I said, I'm no psychiatrist," Melander said. "But it looks as if his wife's death was something he blamed on the whole police force, not just on Nyman and his crowd."

Martin Beck walked back to the door and assumed his favorite position with one arm on the filing cabinet.

"You mean he quite simply rejects a police force where a thing like that can happen," he said.

Melander nodded and sucked on his pipe, which had gone out.

"Yes, at least I can imagine that's roughly the way he reasoned."

"Is anything known about his private life all this time?" asked Martin Beck.

"Not much. He was something of a lone wolf, after all, and didn't have any friends on the force. He gave up officer's training when he got married. He did a good deal of target shooting, but otherwise he didn't take part in any police athletics."

"His personal relationships then? He had a daughter, who ought to be . . . how old now?"

"Eleven," Rönn said.

"Yes," said Melander. "He took care of his daughter himself. They lived in the apartment he and his wife found when they got married."

Melander didn't have any children, but Rönn and Martin Beck pondered the practical difficulties of being a single parent and a policeman on top of it.

"Didn't he have someone to take care of the kid?" said Rönn incredulously. "Like when he was at work, I mean?"

Rönn's son had just turned seven. During those seven years, especially on vacations and weekends, he had often marveled at the fact that at certain periods of its life a single child was capable of occupying the entire time and energy of two full-grown adults virtually twenty-four hours a day.

"Up until 1964 he had the little girl at a day-care center, and since both of his parents were alive, they took care of her when he worked nights."

"Then what?" Rönn said. "After '64?"

"I guess after that we don't know anything about him," said Martin Beck, and looked questioningly at Melander.

"No," Melander said. "He was fired in August that year. No one missed him. Everyone who'd had anything to do with him just wanted to forget him as quickly as possible. For one reason or another."

"Don't we even know what kind of job he got next?" asked Martin Beck.

"He applied for a job as a night watchman in October that same year, but I don't know if he got it. And then he vanishes from our picture."

"When he was fired," Rönn said, "was it just a question of the straw that broke the camel's back?"

"How do you mean?"

"I mean did he have too many demerits, or did he do something in particular?"

"Well the camel's back was ready to break all right, but the direct cause of his dismissal was a breach of discipline. On Friday the seventh of August, Åke Eriksson had the afternoon watch outside the American Embassy. That was 1964, before the big demonstrations against the war in Vietnam had started. As you'll recall, in those days there was only one man on routine watch outside the U.S. Embassy. It wasn't a popular job, it was so dull just wandering back and forth out there."

"But in those days you could still juggle your nightstick," said Martin Beck.

"I remember one guy in particular," Rönn said. "He was fantastic. If Eriksson was as good as that, he maybe got a job in a circus."

Melander threw a tired glance at Rönn. Then he looked at his watch.

"I promised Saga to be home for lunch," he said. "So if I might continue . . ."

"I'm sorry. I just happened to think of that guy," muttered Rönn, offended. "Go on."

"As I was saying, Eriksson was supposed to be watching the embassy, but he just simply said the hell with it. He went out there and relieved the man on the preceding watch. And then he just left. The fact was that a week or so earlier Eriksson had gotten a call to a place on Fredrikshofsgatan where they'd found the janitor dead in the cellar. He'd put a rope around a pipe in the furnace room and hanged himself, and there was no reason to doubt it was suicide. In a locked room in the basement they found a cache of stolen goods—cameras, radios, TV's, furniture, rugs, paintings, a whole bunch of stuff from burglaries committed earlier that year. The janitor had been a fence, and within a few days they'd arrested the men who were using the cellar as a hiding place. Well, all Eriksson really had to do with it was that he'd gone out on the call, and once he and his partner had roped off the area and called in some people from down here, all they had to do was report the suicide and that was that. But Eriksson got the idea that the thing hadn't really been cleared up. As I remember, he thought, for one thing, that the janitor had been murdered, and for another, he was hoping to catch some more members of the gang. So instead of going back to the embassy, which of course he never should have left, he spent the whole afternoon at Fredrikshofsgatan questioning the tenants and snooping around. On an ordinary day maybe no one would even have noticed he wasn't on duty, but as luck would have it one of the first real demonstrations against the embassy took place that very afternoon. Two days before, on the fifth of August, the U.S. had attacked North Vietnam and dropped bombs all up and down the coast, and so now several hundred people had gathered to protest the aggression. Since the demonstration was completely unexpected, the embassy's own security people were taken by surprise, and since on top of that our friend Eriksson was nowhere in sight, it was quite a while before the police arrived in any strength. The demonstration was peaceful, people were chanting slogans and standing around with their picket signs while a delegation went in to deliver a written protest to the ambassador. But as you know, the regular police weren't used to demonstrations and acted the way they always do at a riot, and there was one hell of an uproar. Crowds of people were hauled into the station and some of them had been treated pretty badly. All of this was blamed on Eriksson, and since he was guilty of a grave dereliction of duty he was immediately relieved of his duties and a couple of days later officially dismissed. Exit Åke Eriksson."

Melander stood up.

"And exit Fredrik Melander," he said. "I'm not planning to miss my lunch. I sincerely hope you won't need me again today, but if you do you know where I am."

He put away his tobacco pouch and pipe and got into his coat. Martin Beck walked over and sat down in his chair.

"Do you really think it's Eriksson who cut down Nyman?" said Melander from the door.

Rönn shrugged his shoulders and Martin Beck didn't answer.

"I think it seems unlikely," Melander said. "In that case he should have done it back then when his wife died. Revenge and hate can cool off quite a bit in ten years. You're on the wrong track. But good luck. So long."

He left.

Rönn looked at Martin Beck.

"He's probably right."

Martin Beck sat silently, shuffling at random through the papers on the table.

"I was thinking of something Melander said. About his parents. Maybe they still live where they lived ten years ago."

He started shuffling more purposefully in the pile of documents. Rönn didn't say a word, but he looked at Martin Beck without enthusiasm. Martin Beck finally found what he was looking for.

"Here's the address. Gamla Södertäljevägen in Segeltorp."

23.

The car was a black Plymouth with white fenders and two blue lights on the roof. As if that weren't enough, the four words POLICE, POLICE, POLICE, and POLICE were written on the hood, trunk and both sides in large and extremely legible white letters.

Despite the "B" on the license plate, which meant it was registered outside Stockholm, the car was at the moment moving at a good speed across the city limits at Norrtull. Headed away from the road to Uppsala and, more importantly, away from the Solna police station.

The patrol car was new and well provided with modern equipment, but technical refinements could do nothing significant to improve its crew. This consisted of Patrolmen Karl Kristiansson and Kurt Kvant, two blond giants from Skåne whose nearly twelve years of adventure as radio policemen included several successful and a vast number of entirely unsuccessful actions.

At this particular moment they seemed once again well on their way to trouble.

To be specific, Kristiansson had found himself compelled to arrest the Rump some four minutes earlier. This misfortune could be blamed neither on bad luck nor overzealousness. On the contrary, it had been occasioned by an unusually flagrant and thoughtless provocation.

It had started with Kvant's pulling up and stopping in front of the newsstand at Haga Terminal. He had then taken out his wallet and lent Kristiansson ten crowns, whereupon the latter got out of the car.

Kristiansson was always broke, which was a result of the fact that he squandered all his money on the soccer pools. Only two people knew of this overwhelming mania. One of them was Kvant, since two men in a radio car are very much dependent on each other and can hardly keep secrets except the ones they have in common. The other was Kristiansson's wife, whose

125

name was Kerstin and who suffered from the same ad-
diction. In fact they had even begun to neglect their sex
life, since all of their time together was spent filling in
the soccer coupons and working out incredibly complicated systems based on a combination of calculated
odds and random selections supplied by their two minor
children, aided by a pair of dice manufactured specifi-
cally for this purpose.

At the newsstand, Kristiansson bought copies of
Sports News and two other special newspapers, as well
as a stick of licorice for Kvant. He took the change in
his right hand and stuffed it in his pocket. He held the
papers in his left, and as he turned toward the car he
was already devouring the first page of *All Right* with
his eyes. His mind was completely occupied by the
question of how Millwall, one of his key teams, would
fare in its difficult match against Portsmouth, when he
suddenly heard a wheedling voice behind him.

"You forgot this, Inspector."

Kristiansson felt something brush the sleeve of his
coat, and he automatically drew his right hand from his
pocket and closed his fingers around something strikingly cold and slimy. He gave a start and looked up, to his
horror, directly into the face of the Rump.

Then he looked at the object in his hand.

Karl Kristiansson was very much on duty, standing in
a crowded public place. He was wearing a uniform with
shiny buttons and a shoulder belt, plus a pistol and a
nightstick in white holsters at his waist. In one hand he
was holding a pickled pig's foot.

"To each his own! Hope you like it! Otherwise you
can cram it!" howled the Rump and burst into roaring
laughter.

The Rump was a vagabond beggar and peddler. His
name had been given him for obvious reasons, since the
portion of anatomy in question was quite overwhelming
and made his head, arms and legs look like immaterial
afterthoughts. He was just under five feet tall, that is,
more than a foot shorter than Kristiansson and Kvant.

What made the man so uninviting, however, was not
his physical constitution but his clothing.

The Rump was wearing two long overcoats, three

suit jackets, four pairs of pants and five vests. This means a good fifty pockets, and he was known among other things for carrying considerable amounts of cash, always in coin of the realm and never in denominations larger than ten öre.

Kristiansson and Kvant had apprehended the Rump exactly eleven times but had taken him into the station only twice. Namely, the first two times, and then only due to lack of judgment and experience.

On the first occasion he had had 1,230 one-öre pieces, 2,780 two-öre pieces, 2,037 five-öre pieces and one ten-öring in forty-three pockets. The search had taken three hours and twenty minutes, and at the subsequent trial he was indeed sentenced to pay a fine of ten crowns for insulting an officer of the law, and true enough the pig snout he had affixed to the radiator of the patrol car was confiscated by the crown, but on the other hand Kristiansson and Kvant had been forced to appear as witnesses, and that on their day off.

They weren't so lucky the second time. On that occasion, the Rump had had no less than three hundred and twenty crowns, ninety-three öre in sixty-two pockets. The search had taken all of seven hours, and to make their misery complete he was later found not guilty by an idiotic judge who utterly failed to appreciate the niceties of the *skånsk* idiom and could hear nothing disparaging or slanderous in the expressions *fubbick mögbör*, *gåsapick* and *puggasole*. When Kvant, with great difficulty, managed to translate *mögbör* (to "vehicle for the transport of fertilizer"), the judge had remarked sourly that it was Kristiansson and not the patrol car who was the plaintiff, and that the court considered it as good as impossible to insult a Plymouth sedan, particularly not by comparing it with some other practical conveyance.

The Rump, like Kristiansson and Kvant, emanated from the plains of southern Sweden and knew how to choose his words.

When in addition Kvant happened to call the defendant "the Rump" instead of Carl Fredrik Gustaf Oscar Jönsson-Käck, the day was irretrievably lost. The judge threw the case out and admonished Kvant to avoid the use of doubtful and enigmatic dialectical invective in open court.

And now it was all about to begin again.

Kristiansson looked around surreptitiously and saw nothing but happily expectant or already openly cackling citizens.

To make matters worse, the Rump now extracted an additional pig's foot from one of his inner pockets.

"This here's from one of your relatives and buddies who went to his reward the other day," he shouted. "His last wish was it should go to somebody who's as big a swine as he was. And that he'd see you soon where every fucking pig winds up. In the big lard bucket in hell."

Kristiansson's perplexed blue eyes sought out Kvant, but he was looking the other way, thereby indicating that all of this had little or nothing to do with him.

"You look real good with hoofs, Inspector," said the Rump. "But it looks like you're missing your curly tail. Don't worry, we'll fix that up."

He inserted his free hand into his wardrobe.

Cheerful faces were now visible on every side, and some unidentifiable person on the edge of the crowd added his two cents worth in a loud voice.

"Right on," he said. "Give the bastard what's coming to him."

The Rump was troubled by Kristiansson's obvious uncertainty.

"Fucking cop!" he screeched. "Sow-hole! Hog-prick! Cunt-licker!"

An expectant rustle swelled in the crowd.

Kristiansson stuck out the pig's foot in order to grab hold of his antagonist. At the same time, he was searching desperately for a way out. He could already hear thousands of copper coins clanking in secret pockets.

"He's putting his paws on me," howled the Rump.

With well-feigned anguish.

"On me, a poor invalid. The cock-sucker's laying hands on an honest peddler, just because I showed him a little human kindness. Let me go, you fucking son of a bitch!"

When it came right down to it, Kristiansson was handicapped by the pig's foot and unable to carry out any specific act of violence, but the Rump facilitated matters by jerking open the door of the police car and leaping into the back seat before Kristiansson had time to make use of his somewhat inappropriate weapon.

Kvant didn't even turn his head.

"How the hell could you be such an idiot, Karl?" he said. "Falling right into his hands like that? This is all your fault."

He started the motor.

"Jesus," said Kristiansson, not very constructively.

"Where does he want to go?" Kvant asked furiously.

"Solnavägen ninety-two," squeaked the prisoner happily.

The Rump was by no means dumb. He asked to be taken to the precinct central station. He was looking forward with ill-concealed delight to getting his coins counted.

"We can't dump him anywhere in our precinct," Kvant said. "It's too risky."

"Drive me to the station," the Rump entreated them. "Call them on the radio and tell them we're coming so they can put on the coffeepot. I can have a cup while you start counting."

He shook himself to make his point.

And sure enough. An enormous number of copper coins rattled and clattered ominously from a profusion of secret hiding places beneath his clothes.

Searching the Rump was the job of whatever man or men had been foolish enough to bring him in. That was an unwritten but nevertheless inflexible rule.

"Ask him where he wants to go," Kvant said.

"You just asked him that yourself," said Kristiansson peevishly.

"I wasn't the one who picked him up," Kvant retorted. "I never even saw him till he got in the car."

One of Kvant's specialties was seeing nothing and hearing nothing.

Kristiansson knew of only one way to touch the Rump's human frailty. He rattled the change in his pocket.

"How much?" the Rump asked greedily.

Kristiansson pulled out his change from the ten and looked at it.

"Six fifty at least."

"That's bribery," the prisoner complained.

The strictly legal aspects of this were a mystery to both Kristiansson and Kvant. Had *he* offered *them* money, it would have been a clear attempt to suborn a civil servant. But this was the other way around.

"Anyway, six fifty isn't enough. I need money for a bottle of Dessert Wine."

Kvant took out his wallet and peeled off another ten. The Rump took it.

"Drop me off at a liquor store," he said.

"Not here in Solna," said Kvant. "That's too much of a risk, dammit."

"Then take me to Sigtunagatan. They know me there, and I've got some buddies in Vasa Park, down by the johns."

"We can't just drop him off right in front of the liquor store, for Christ's sake," said Kristiansson anxiously.

They drove south past the post office and Tennstopet and on down Dalagatan.

"I'll take a swing into the park here," Kvant said. "Drive in a ways and let him out."

"Hey, you never paid me for the pig's feet," said the Rump.

They didn't hit him. Their physical superiority was much too obvious, and then too they weren't in the habit of hitting people, at least not without cause.

Moreover, neither of them was a particularly zealous policeman. Kvant almost always reported whatever he happened to see and hear, but he managed to see and hear exceedingly little. Kristiansson was more an out-and-out slacker who simply ignored everything that might cause complications or unnecessary trouble.

Kvant turned into the park alongside the Eastman Institute. The trees were bare and the park was sad and empty. As soon as he'd made the turn, he stopped.

"Get out here, Karl. I'll drive on in a ways and drop him off as quietly as I can. If you see anything that looks like trouble, blow your whistle, the usual signal."

The car smelled, as always, of sweaty feet and old vomit, but even more strongly at the moment of cheap alcohol and body odor from the prisoner.

Kristiansson nodded and got out. He left his newspapers in the back seat but still held the pig's foot in his right hand.

The car disappeared behind him. He walked up toward the street and at first saw nothing that looked in the least like trouble. But he felt uneasy somehow, and waited impatiently for Kvant to come back with the car so they could retreat to the peace and security of their own precinct. He'd have to listen to Kvant bitch about his wife, her physical inadequacy and her fierce temper, until their watch was over. But he was used to that. For his part, he liked his own wife fine, particularly in regard to this business with the soccer pools, and he seldom mentioned her.

Kvant seemed to be taking his time. He probably didn't want to risk being seen, or else maybe the Rump had upped the price.

In front of the steps up to the Eastman Institute there was a sort of open space, with a round stone fountain or whatever it was in the middle. On the other side of this stood a black Volkswagen, parked so obviously in violation of the law that not even as lazy a policeman as Kristiansson could avoid reacting.

He wasn't exactly thinking of doing anything about it, but the minutes were dragging, so he started strolling slowly around the circular basin. He could at least pretend to be having a look at this car whose owner seemed to think he could park continental-style right in the middle of the capital of Sweden, Land of Prohibitions. Walking up and looking at a parked car doesn't place you under any obligation after all.

The decorative fountain was about twelve feet in diameter, and as Kristiansson got to the other side he thought he saw the sun dazzle for an instant in a window high up in the building across the street.

A fraction of a second later he heard a short, sharp report and at the same instant something hit him like a hammer in the right knee. The leg seemed to disappear beneath him. He staggered and fell backward over the

stone balustrade and down into the basin of the fountain, the bottom of which, at this time of year, was covered with spruce twigs, rotting leaves and litter.

He lay on his back and heard himself scream.

He was dimly aware of several more echoing explo-
sions, but apparently none of them were aimed at him.

He still held the pig's foot in one hand and had not
succeeded in connecting the muzzle flash with the report, nor with the bullet that had crushed the bone just
below his knee.

24.

Gunvald Larsson still had his eyes on the hands of
his watch when he heard the second shot. It was followed immediately by at least four more.

Like most watches in the country, his showed common standard Swedish time, that is, fifteen degrees or
one hour East Greenwich, and since it was well-cared-
for and neither lost nor gained as much as one second a
year, his observations were exact.

The first shot was heard at precisely twelve ten. The
next four, possibly five, all came in the course of two
seconds, that is, between the fourth and the sixth second
from the starting point. Which was twelve ten.

Guided by commendable instinct and a correct as-
sessment of direction and distance, Gunvald Larsson
and Kollberg acted together during the next two minutes.

They jumped into the nearest car, which happened to
be Gunvald Larsson's red BMW.

Gunvald Larsson hit the starter, peeled some rubber
and raced off—not the way he had come, around the
central hospital, but past the old heating plant and
along the narrow drive that wound up toward Dalagatan between the maternity ward and the Eastman Institute. Then he turned one hundred and eighty degrees to
the left and out onto the flagstone court in front of the
Institute, braked hard, skidded, and came to a stop with

the car slightly at an angle between the fountain and the broad stone steps to the building.

Even before they had time to open the doors and get out, both Gunvald Larsson and Kollberg saw that a uniformed policeman was lying on his back among the spruce branches in the basin. They also saw that he was wounded but alive, and that there were a number of other people in the area. Of these, three were lying on the ground, wounded, dead or trying to find cover, and the rest were standing still, probably wherever they had found themselves when the shots were fired. A patrol car was just coming to a stop on the road up out of Vasa Park. There was a patrolman at the wheel and he started to open the left front door even before the car had come to a halt.

They got out simultaneously, Gunvald Larsson on the left and Kollberg on the right.

Gunvald Larsson didn't hear the next shot, but he saw his Chinese fur hat leave his head and land on the steps, and he suddenly felt as if someone had drawn a red-hot poker along the hairline from his right temple to a point just above his ear. He hadn't even had time to straighten up, and now his head was knocked to one side and he heard a shot and a shrill whistling, a dry crack and a whining ricochet, and then in two huge leaps he flung himself up the eight steps and pressed himself against the stone wall to the left of the entranceway with its three rectangular pillars. He put his hand to his cheek and it came away covered with blood. The bullet had plowed a furrow in his scalp. The wound was bleeding copiously and his kid jacket was ruined. Already, and for good.

Kollberg reacted as quickly as Gunvald Larsson. He ducked back into the car and was quick-witted enough to vault over into the back seat. Immediately afterward, two shots cracked through the roof of the car and burned into the stuffing of the front seat. He could see Gunvald Larsson in the entranceway, flat up against the wall and apparently wounded. He knew he had to get out of the car and up the steps at once, and in an almost reflex action he kicked open the right-hand front door with his foot and at the same time hurled himself out through the left-hand rear. Three shots, all aimed at the right side of the car, but Kollberg was already outside on the left where he grabbed hold of the first of the four iron handrails, swung himself up the eight steps without even touching them, and landed with his head and right shoulder in Gunvald Larsson's gut.

Then he took a deep breath, struggled to his feet and pressed himself against the wall beside Gunvald Larsson, who was grunting oddly, probably from surprise or lack of air.

Nothing happened for several seconds, maybe five or ten. Apparently a brief cease-fire.

The wounded patrolman still lay in the fountain, and his partner stood by the radio car with his pistol in his right hand and looked around dumfoundedly. He probably hadn't seen Kollberg and Gunvald Larsson and lacked any sort of general view of the situation. But in any case he did see his wounded buddy, twenty-five feet from where he stood, and he started walking toward him, still with a perplexed expression on his face and his service revolver in his fist.

"What in hell are those two blockheads doing here?" muttered Gunvald Larsson.

And then a second later yelled, "Kvant! Stop! Cover!"

Where? Kollberg wondered.

Because there wasn't any cover.

Gunvald Larsson appeared to have realized the same thing, because he didn't yell again. And for the moment nothing happened except that the blond patrolman straightened up and stared in the direction of the entranceway and then went on walking. Apparently he couldn't distinguish the two men in the shadows.

A red double-decker bus drove past headed south on Dalagatan. Someone screamed hysterically for help.

The patrolman had reached the fountain, put one knee on the rim and leaned down over the wounded man.

There was a little ledge on the inside of the stone basin, presumably for small children to sit on during the summer and splash their bare feet in the water. His leather jacket gleamed in the sun as the policeman laid his pistol on the ledge to free his hands. He turned his broad back upward toward the sky, and the two rifle bullets struck him less than a second apart, the first in the back of the neck and the other directly between his shoulder blades.

Kurt Kvant fell at right angles on top of his partner. He didn't make a sound. Kristiansson had had time to see the exit wound made by the first bullet as it emerged neatly halfway between Kvant's Adam's apple and his collar. Then he felt the weight of Kvant's body across his own hips, and then he passed out, from pain, and fear, and loss of blood. They lay in a cross on the spruce branches, one of them unconscious and the other one dead.

"God damn," said Gunvald Larsson. "God damn it to hell!"

Kollberg was seized by a strong sense of unreality.

He had been waiting for something to happen. Now something was happening, but it was as if it were taking place in another dimension from the one where he himself still lived and moved.

Something else happened. Someone moved, walked into the magic flagstone square. A little boy with a moss-green quilted jacket, blotchy jeans in various shades of blue, and green galoshes with reflecting tape. Blond curly hair. He couldn't have been more than five. The boy walked slowly and hesitantly toward the fountain.

Kollberg felt the quivering in his body, the automatic physical preparation for rushing out of the doorway and picking up the child in his arms. Gunvald Larsson noticed it too, and without taking his eyes from the macabre scene before them, he put his large bloody hand on Kollberg's chest.

"Wait," he said.

The boy stood by the edge of the basin and stared down at the crossed bodies. Then he stuck his left thumb in his mouth, put his right hand to his left ear, and burst into tears.

Stood for a moment with the tears trickling down his

plump cheeks, his head on one side. Turned suddenly and ran back the way he'd come. Across the sidewalk and the street. Out of the flagstone quadrangle. Back to the land of the living.

No one shot at him.

Gunvald Larsson looked at his watch.

Twelve twelve and twenty-seven.

"Two minutes and twenty-seven seconds," he said to himself.

And Kollberg thought, by association but a little oddly: Two minutes and twenty-seven seconds, not generally thought to be a very long time. But in certain contexts it could mean a lot. A good Swedish sprinter, Björn Malmroos for example, could theoretically run the hundred meters fourteen times. That's a lot.

Two patrolmen shot, one of them already dead for sure. In all probability the other one too.

Gunvald Larsson a quarter of an inch from death. Two inches himself.

And then the little boy in the moss-green jacket.

That's also a lot.

Lennart Kollberg looked at his own watch.

It already said twenty past.

In certain other respects he was a perfectionist, but in some circumstances he simply didn't make it.

On the other hand, it was an Exakta, a Russian watch, and he'd bought it for sixty-three crowns. It had been running nicely for over three years, and if you set it and wound it at regular intervals it even told the time.

Gunvald Larsson's chronometer had cost 1,500 crowns.

Kollberg lifted his hands, looked at them, and cupped them around his mouth.

"Hello! Hello!" he roared. "Anyone who can hear me! The area is dangerous! Take cover!"

He took a deep breath and started again.

"Attention! This is the police! The area is dangerous! Take cover!"

Gunvald Larsson turned his head and looked at him. The expression in his china-blue eyes was peculiar.

Then Gunvald Larsson looked at the door leading

into the Institute. It would of course be locked on a Saturday. The entire big stone building was undoubtedly empty. He eased closer to the door and kicked it in with superhuman strength.

It should have been impossible, but he did it. Kollberg followed him into the building. The next door was unlocked and made of glass, but he kicked in that one too. Splinters flew.

They came to a telephone.

Gunvald Larsson picked up the receiver, dialed 90-000 and asked for emergency.

"This is Gunvald Larsson. There's a madman in the building at Dalagatan thirty-four. He's shooting from the roof or the top floor with an automatic weapon. There are two dead patrolmen lying in the fountain in front of the Eastman Institute. Alert all the central precincts. Block off Dalagatan and Västmannagatan from Norra Bantorget to Karlbergsvägen, and Odengatan from Odenplan to St. Eriksplan. And all the cross streets in the area west of Västmannagatan and south of Karlbergsvägen. Have you got that? What? Notify command? Yes, notify everybody. But wait a minute. Don't send any patrol cars to that address. And no one in uniform. We'll assemble at . . ."

He lowered the receiver and frowned.

"Odenplan," said Kollberg.

"Right," said Gunvald Larsson. "Odenplan'll be fine. What? I'm inside the Eastman Institute. In a few minutes I'll go over and try to take him."

He banged down the receiver and went into the nearest washroom. Wet a towel and wiped the blood off his face. Took another and tied it around his head. Spots of blood appeared immediately on the provisional bandage.

Then he unbuttoned his kid jacket and his coat. And drew his pistol, which he carried clipped to his belt. He examined it grimly, then looked at Kollberg.

"What kind of a weapon you got?"

Kollberg shook his head.

"Oh that's right," said Gunvald Larsson. "You're some sort of a pacifist."

His pistol, like all his possessions, was not like other people's. A Smith & Wesson 38 Master, which he'd bought because he didn't like the standard Swedish police model, the 7.65 mm Walther.

"You know what?" said Gunvald Larsson. "I've always thought you were a fucking idiot."

Kollberg nodded.

"How did you figure we'd get across the street?" he said.

25.

The house in Segeltorp could hardly be called imposing—a little wooden building which, to judge from the architecture, had been built as a summer house at least fifty years before. The original paint was worn clear through to gray wood in places, but it was still apparent that the house had once been bright yellow with white trim. The fence around the yard, which seemed large in proportion to the house, had been painted Falun red not so very many years ago. As had the handrail on the steps, the outer door and the latticework around a small verandah.

It stood quite some distance above the highway, and since the gate was open Rönn drove up the steep drive all the way to the back of the house.

Martin Beck got out immediately and took several deep breaths while he looked around. He felt a little ill, as he often did when he rode in a car.

The yard was neglected and full of weeds. A partially overgrown path led to an old rusted sundial that looked pathetic and out of place on its cement pedestal surrounded by scrubby bushes.

Rönn slammed the door to the car.

"I'm starting to get a little hungry," he said. "Think we've got time for a quick bite when we're through here?"

Martin Beck looked at his watch. Rönn was used to

eating lunch at this time of day, it was already ten minutes after twelve. Martin Beck was careless about meals himself. He didn't really like to eat while he was working and preferred having his dinner in the evening.

"Sure," he said. "Come on, let's go in."

They walked around the corner of the house, up the steps and knocked at the door. It was opened immediately by a man in his seventies.

"Come in," he said.

He stood silently by and looked at them inquiringly as they hung up their coats in the crowded front hall.

"Come in," he said again, and stood to one side so they could pass.

There were two doors at the other end of the front hall. One of them led through a short hall to the kitchen. From this second hall, a stairway led up to the second floor or attic. The other door led into the living room. The air inside was damp and stale, and rather dim because of the tall fernlike potted plants that stood in the windowsills and kept out most of the daylight.

"Please sit down," said the man. "My wife will be right here. With some coffee."

The room was dominated by a set of peasant-style furniture—a straight-backed pine sofa and four chairs with striped upholstered seats around a large table topped by a massive slab of beautifully veined fir. Martin Beck and Rönn sat down at opposite ends of the sofa. A door stood ajar at the far end of the room, and through it they could see the cracked end of a mahogany bedstead and a wardrobe with oval mirrors on its doors. The man walked over and closed the door before sitting down in one of the chairs on the other side of the table.

He was thin and bent, and the skin on his face and bald head was gray and covered with light brown liver spots. He was wearing a thick handknit sweater over a gray-and-black checked flannel shirt.

"I was just saying to my wife when we heard the car that you gentlemen made very good time. I wasn't sure my directions were so good on the phone."

"It wasn't hard to find," Rönn said.

"No, that's right, you're policemen, so you know your way around—in town and out. Åke got to know the city awfully well from being a policeman."

He took out a flattened pack of John Silvers and held it out. Martin Beck and Rönn both shook their heads.

"Well, it was to talk about Åke you gentlemen came," said the man. "Like I told you on the phone, I really don't know what time he left. Mother and I thought he might stay the night, but he must have gone home instead. He often stays overnight. It's his birthday today, so we thought he'd stay and have breakfast in bed."

"Does he have a car?" Rönn asked.

"Oh yes, he's got a Volks. Here's Mother with the coffee."

He stood up when his wife came in from the kitchen. She was carrying a tray and put it down on the table. Then she dried her hands on her skirt and shook hands with the two guests.

"Mrs. Eriksson," she said when they stood up and said their names.

She served the coffee and put the tray on the floor, then sat down next to her husband and folded her hands in her lap. She looked to be about the same age as he. Her hair was silver gray, severely permed into small stiff curls, but her round face was almost completely wrinkle-free and the red color in her cheeks didn't look like makeup. She stared down at her hands, and when she suddenly threw a timid glance at Martin Beck he wondered if she were afraid or simply shy with strangers.

"There are a few questions we'd like to ask you about your son, Mrs. Eriksson," he said. "If I understood your husband correctly, he was here last night. Do you know what time he left?"

She looked at her husband as if hoping he would answer for her, but he stirred his coffee and said nothing.

"No," she said hesitantly. "I don't know. I guess he left after we'd gone to bed."

"And when was that?"

She looked at her husband again.

"Yes, what time was that, Otto?"

"Ten thirty. Eleven maybe. We usually go to bed earlier, but since Åke was here . . . I guess it was probably closer to ten thirty."

"So you didn't hear him go?"

"No," the man said. "But why do you want to know? Has anything happened to him?"

"No," said Martin Beck. "Not as far as we know. This is just routine. Tell me, what's your son doing these days?"

The woman had gone back to staring at her hands, and her husband answered.

"He's still repairing elevators. It's a year now since he started that."

"And before that?"

"Oh, he did a little of everything. He was with a plumbing firm for a while, and then he used to drive a taxi, and he's been a night watchman, and just before he went to work for this elevator company he drove a truck. That was while he was training for this new thing, this elevator thing."

"When he was here last night," said Martin Beck, "did he seem himself? What did he talk about?"

The man didn't answer right away, and the woman took a cookie and started breaking it into small pieces on her plate.

"I guess he was pretty much like always," said the man finally. "He didn't say much, but he never does any more. I guess he was worried about the rent, and then this business with Malin."

"Malin?" said Rönn.

"Yes, his little girl. They took his little girl away. And now he's going to lose his apartment too."

"Excuse me," said Martin Beck. "I don't quite understand. Who took his daughter away from him? I assume it's his daughter you mean?"

"Yes, Malin," said the man, and patted his wife on the arm. "She was named after my mother. I thought you knew that. That the Child Welfare Board took Malin away from Åke."

"Why?" asked Martin Beck.

"Why did the police murder his wife?"

"Please answer the question," said Martin Beck. "Why did they take the child away from him?"

"Oh they've tried before, and now they finally managed to get some sort of paper that says he can't take care of her. We offered to take her here, of course, but we're too old they said. And this house isn't good enough."

The woman looked at Martin Beck, but when he met her glance she looked quickly down into her coffee cup. And then she spoke up, quietly but indignantly.

"As if it was better for her to live with strangers. And anyway this is better than in the city."

"You've taken care of your granddaughter before, haven't you?"

"Yes, many times," the woman said. "There's a room in the attic where she can stay when she's here. Åke's old room."

"The kinds of jobs Åke's had, he couldn't always take care of her," the man said. "They thought he was unstable, whatever that means. That he couldn't hold a job, I think that's what they meant. That's not so easy these days. Unemployment just gets worse and worse all the time. But he's always been so good to Malin."

"When did all this happen?" asked Martin Beck.

"With Malin? They came and got her the day before yesterday."

"Was he very upset about it last night?" Rönn asked.

"Yes, I guess he was, though he didn't say much about it. Then there was this thing about the rent too, but there's no way we can help him with our little pension."

"Couldn't he pay his rent?"

"No. And now they're about to evict him, he said. With rents so high it's a wonder people can afford to live anyplace."

"Where does he live?"

"On Dalagatan. In a brand-new building. He couldn't find anything else when they tore down the place he was living before. And he was making better money then, of course, so he figured he could make it. But that doesn't matter so much. The worst part was this thing with his little girl."

"I'd like to know a little more about this business with the Child Welfare people," said Martin Beck. "They don't just take a child away from its father, not just like that."

"Don't they?"

"They claim, at least, that they make a thorough investigation first."

"Yes, I suppose so. Some people came out here and talked to the wife and me and looked at the house and asked all sorts of questions about Ake. He wasn't very happy, not after Marja died, but you can understand that, I guess. They said his depression—that he was so gloomy all the time—had an injurious effect on the child's mental state. I remember that's what they said, they always have to talk so fine. And that it wasn't good he had so many different jobs and such funny hours. Yes, and then he had money troubles, couldn't pay the rent and so forth, and then, of course, there were some of his neighbors in the building who complained to the Child Welfare that he left Malin alone too much at night and that she didn't eat properly and so on."

"Do you know who else they talked to?"

"The people he'd worked for. I think they tried to get hold of every boss he'd ever had."

"The ones in the police department too?"

"Yes of course. That was the most important one. Apparently."

"And apparently he didn't give him much of a recommendation," said Martin Beck.

"No, Ake said he wrote some sort of a letter that absolutely ruined his chances of keeping Malin."

"Do you know who it was that wrote this letter?" asked Martin Beck.

"Yes. It was that Inspector Nyman, the same one who let Ake's wife lie there and die without lifting a finger."

Martin Beck and Rönn exchanged a quick glance.

Mrs. Eriksson looked from her husband to them, anxious about how they would react to this new accusation. This one was directed at one of their colleagues after all. She held out the cake dish, first to Rönn, who helped himself to a thick slab of sponge cake, then to Martin Beck, who shook his head.

"Did your son talk about Inspector Nyman when he was here last night?"

"He just said it was his fault that they'd taken Malin. Nothing else. He's not very talkative, our Åke, but last night he was quieter than usual. Wasn't he, Karin?"

"Yes," said his wife, poking at some crumbs on her plate.

"What did he do while he was here? Last night, I mean," said Martin Beck.

"He had dinner with us. Then we watched TV for a while. Then he went up to his room and we went to bed."

Martin Beck had noticed the telephone in the front hall as they came in.

"Did he use the phone at any time during the evening?" he asked.

"Why are you asking all these questions?" the woman said. "Has Åke done anything?"

"I'm afraid I have to ask you to just please answer our questions first," said Martin Beck. "Did he make any calls from here last night?"

The couple across from him sat silent for a moment.

"Maybe," the man said then. "I don't know. Åke can use the phone any time he wants to after all."

"So you didn't hear him talking on the phone."

"No. We were watching TV. I think I remember he went out for a while and closed the door behind him, and he doesn't usually do that if he's just going to the toilet. The phone's in the hall, and if the TV's on you have to close the door so you won't be disturbed. We don't hear so well either, so we usually have the sound up pretty high."

"What time would that have been? That he used the phone, I mean?"

"I don't really know. But we were watching a movie, and that was right in the middle of it. About nine, maybe. Why do you want to know?"

Martin Beck didn't answer. Rönn had gobbled down the sponge cake and now suddenly spoke up.

"Your son's a very good shot, as I recall. Among the best in the department at that time. Do you know if he still has any guns?"

The woman looked at Rönn with something new in her eyes, and the man straightened up proudly. It would probably be easy to count the number of times in the last ten years these people had heard anyone praise their son.

"Yes," the man said. "Åke's won a lot of prizes. We don't have them here, unfortunately. He keeps them in his apartment on Dalagatan. And as for guns . . ."

"He ought to sell those things," the woman said. "They were so expensive, and he's short of money."

"Do you know what guns he's got?" Rönn asked.

"Yes," the man said. "I do. Did a lot of target shooting myself when I was younger. First of all, Åke's got his weapons from the Home Guard or the Civil Defense or whatever they call it these days. He took night courses and got a commission too, not bad, if I do say so myself."

"Do you know what kinds of weapons?" said Rönn stubbornly.

"First of all, his Mauser rifle. And then his pistol, he's terrific with a pistol, won his first gold medal years ago."

"What kind of pistol?"

"Hammerli International. He showed it to me. And then he's got . . ."

The man hesitated.

"Got what?"

"I don't know . . . he's got a license for those two I mentioned, of course, as you gentlemen realize . . ."

"I assure you we're not thinking of arresting your son for illegal possession of weapons," said Martin Beck. "What else does he have?"

"An American automatic rifle. Johnson. But he must have a license for that one too, because I know he's entered competitions with it."

"Not a bad arsenal," Martin Beck muttered.

"What else?" said Rönn.

"His old carbine from the Home Guard. But that's not worth much. For that matter it's upstairs in the closet. But the bore is worn, and then those carbines never were much good. But I think that's the only one he keeps up here. He certainly doesn't have all his other things here."

"No, he keeps them at home of course," Rönn said.

"Yes, I suppose he does," the man said. "Of course he's still got his room upstairs here, but naturally he's got all his important stuff at home on Dalagatan. Well, if they won't let him stay in that nice apartment he can always move back in here until he can find something else. It isn't very big, the attic I mean."

"Would you mind if we took a look at his room?" said Martin Beck.

The man looked at him uncertainly.

"No, I guess that's all right. But there's not much to see."

The woman stood up and brushed cake crumbs from her skirt.

"Oh my," she said. "I haven't even been up there today. It may be in a mess."

"It's not so bad," her husband said. "I looked in this morning to see if Åke had slept there last night, and it didn't look so bad at all. Åke's very neat."

The man looked away and went on talking in a lower voice.

"Åke's a good boy. It's not his fault he's had a hard life. We've worked all our lives and tried to raise him as good as we could. But everything went wrong, for him and for us. When I was a young worker I had something to believe in, I thought everything would be fine. Now we're old and no one bothers about us and everything's all wrong. If we'd known what society was coming to, we wouldn't have had any children at all. But they've just been leading us on all these years."

"Who?" said Rönn.

"The politicians. The party bosses. The ones we thought were on our side. Just gangsters, all of them."

"Please show us the room," said Martin Beck.

"Yes," the man said.

He walked ahead of them out into the hall and up a steep, creaking wooden staircase. Right at the top of the stairs was a door, which he opened.

"This is Ake's room. Of course it was nicer looking when he was a boy and lived at home, but he took most of the furniture when he got married and moved away. He's here so seldom now."

He stopped and held open the door, and Martin Beck and Rönn walked into the little attic room. There was a window in the sloping roof, and the walls were covered with faded flowered wallpaper. In one wall was a door covered with the same paper, probably to a closet or a storage room. A narrow folding bed with a gray army blanket for a spread stood against the wall. From the ceiling hung a pale yellow lampshade with a long dirty fringe.

On the wall above the bed there was a small picture in a frame with a broken piece of glass. It depicted a little golden-haired girl sitting in a green meadow and holding a lamb in her arms. Under the foot of the bed was a pink plastic pot.

There was an open weekly magazine and a ballpoint pen on the table, and someone had thrown down an ordinary white kitchen towel with a red border onto one of the wooden chairs.

There was nothing else in the room.

Martin Beck picked up the towel. It was worn thin from many washings and was somewhat stained. He held it up against the light. The stains were yellow and reminded him of the fat that comes on genuine pâté de foie gras. The shape of the stains suggested that someone had wiped off a knife on the towel. The yellow fat made the linen almost transparent, and Martin Beck rubbed the material thoughtfully between his fingers before bringing it to his nose to smell. At the very moment that he realized what the stains consisted of and how they had come about, Rönn interrupted him.

"Look here, Martin," he said.

He was standing by the table, pointing at the magazine. Martin Beck leaned down and saw that something had been written with a ballpoint pen in the upper margin above the crossword puzzle on the right-hand page. Nine names, arranged in three groups.

The names were unevenly printed, and had been gone over several times. His gaze locked on the first column.

STIG OSCAR NYMAN †
PALMON HARALD HULT †
MARTIN BECK †

He managed to notice that among the other names were those of Melander, the Superintendent, the National Chief of Police. And Kollberg.

Then he turned to the man by the door. He stood with his hand on the doorknob and looked at them questioningly.

"Where on Dalagatan does your son live?" said Martin Beck.

"Thirty-four," said the man. "But——"

"Go down to your wife," Martin Beck interrupted him. "We'll be right there."

The man went slowly down the stairs. On the bottom step he turned around and looked in bewilderment at Martin Beck, who waved at him to go on into the living room. Then he turned to Rönn.

"Call Strömgren or whoever the hell's there. Give them the number here and tell him to get in touch right away with Kollberg at Mount Sabbath and tell him to call here immediately. Have you got anything in the car so we can take some prints up here?"

"Yes, sure," Rönn said.

"Good. But make that call first."

Rönn went down to the telephone in the hall.

Martin Beck looked around the cramped little attic room. Then he looked at his watch. Ten minutes to one. He heard Rönn come up the stairs in three great leaps.

Martin Beck looked at Rönn's pale cheeks and unnaturally wide-open eyes and knew that the catastrophe he'd waited for all day had taken place.

26.

Kollberg and Gunvald Larsson were still inside the Eastman Institute when the sirens began their chorus. First they heard the sound of a single vehicle that seemed to come from Kungsholm and drive across St. Erik's Bridge. Then other cars in other parts of the city joined the song; their howling seemed to come from every direction, it filled the air but never came really close.

They found themselves in the center of a silent circle. Something like walking out onto a meadow on a summer night and the crickets stop chirping all around you but only right where you're standing, Kollberg thought.

He had just taken a look out toward Dalagatan and noted that nothing had changed for the worse, while a few things had gotten better. The two policemen still lay in the round basin, but there were no other dead or wounded on the street. The people who'd been there before had disappeared, even the ones who'd been lying on the ground. So apparently they'd not been wounded.

Gunvald Larsson still hadn't answered the question about how they were going to get across the street. Instead, he was chewing thoughtfully on his lower lip and staring past Kollberg at a row of white dentist's smocks hanging on hooks along one wall.

The alternatives were obvious.

Go straight across the flagstone square and across the street, or sneak out through one of the windows onto Vasa Park and take a detour.

Neither one seemed very appealing. The first was a little too much like suicide, and the second took too much time.

Kollberg looked out again, carefully and without moving the curtains.

He nodded toward the fountain with its somewhat surreal ornamentation—a globe with a child kneeling on Scandinavia and two crossed policemen.

"Did you know those two?" he asked.

"Yes," said Gunvald Larsson. "Radio patrolmen from Solna. Kristiansson and Kvant."

Silence for a moment.

"What were they doing here?"

And then Kollberg asked a more interesting question.

"And why should anyone want to shoot them?"

"Why does anyone want to shoot us?"

That was a good question too.

Someone obviously took a great interest in the matter. Someone equipped with an automatic rifle with which he'd dropped two uniformed patrolmen and done his very best to shoot down Kollberg and Gunvald Larsson. But someone who didn't seem to care to shoot at anyone else, despite the fact that to start with there'd been plenty of live targets.

Why?

One answer presented itself immediately. Whoever did the shooting had recognized Kollberg and Gunvald Larsson. He knew who they were and really wanted to kill them.

Had whoever it was also recognized Kristiansson and Kvant? Not necessarily, but the uniforms made them easy to identify. As what?

"It seems to be someone who doesn't like policemen," muttered Kollberg.

"Mmm," said Gunvald Larsson.

He weighed the pistol in his hand.

"Did you see if the bastard was up on the roof or in one of the apartments?" he asked.

"No," said Kollberg. "I really didn't have time to look."

Something happened out on the street. Rather prosaic, but remarkable all the same.

An ambulance rolled up from the south. It stopped, backed up toward the fountain and stopped again. Two men in white coats got out, opened the back doors and pulled out two stretchers. They moved calmly and didn't seem to be the least bit nervous. One of them glanced up toward the nine-story building on the other side of the street. Nothing happened.

Kollberg grimaced.

"Yes," said Gunvald Larsson immediately. "There's our chance."

"Dandy chance," said Kollberg.

He didn't feel particularly enthusiastic, but Gunvald Larsson had already taken off his kid jacket and suit coat and was searching energetically through the white smocks.

"I'm going to try it anyway," he said. "This one looks pretty big."

"They only make three sizes," said Kollberg.

Gunvald Larsson nodded, clipped his pistol to his belt and wriggled into the smock. It was very tight across the shoulders.

Kollberg shook his head and reached out his arm for the largest smock in sight. It was too tight. Across the stomach.

He had a strong feeling that they looked like a pair of comics out of a silent film.

"I think maybe it'll work," said Gunvald Larsson.

"Maybe is the word," said Kollberg.

"Okay?"

"Okay."

They walked down the steps, across the stone pavement and past the ambulance crew, who had just lifted Kvant onto the first stretcher.

Kollberg glanced down at the dead man's face. He recognized him. A patrolman he'd seen a few times at long intervals, and who had once done something notable. What? Captured a dangerous sex criminal? Something like that.

Gunvald Larsson was already halfway across the street. He looked very odd in his ill-fitting doctor's coat and a white rag around his head. The two ambulance attendants stared after him in astonishment.

A shot rang out.

Kollberg ran across the street.

But this time it wasn't aimed at him.

A black-and-white police car was moving east along Odengatan with its siren on. The first shot came just as it passed Sigtunagatan, and it was followed at once by a whole series. Gunvald Larsson took a couple of steps out onto the sidewalk to get a better look. At first the

car sped up, then it started to wobble and skid. The fir
ing had stopped by the time it passed the intersection o
Odengatan and Dalagatan and disappeared. Immediate
ly afterward came an ominous crash of metal agains
metal.

"Idiots," said Gunvald Larsson.

He joined Kollberg in the entranceway, ripped open
his white coat and drew his pistol.

"He's on the roof, that's for sure. Now we'll see."

"Yes, he's on the roof now," Kollberg said.

"What do you mean?"

"I don't think he was on the roof before."

"We'll see," repeated Gunvald Larsson.

The building had two entrances on the street side.
This was the one on the north, and they took it first.
The elevator wasn't working and there were several
nervous tenants on the stairs.

The sight of Gunvald Larsson in a torn coat, bloody
bandage, pistol in hand didn't ease their fears. Kollberg
had his identification in the pocket of his coat, and his
coat was back in the building across the street. If Gunvald Larsson was carrying any papers, he conscien-
tiously avoided showing them.

"Out of the way," he said gruffly.

"Stick together down on the ground floor here,"
Kollberg suggested.

It wasn't so easy to calm them down, these people—
three women, a child and an older man. They'd probably seen what had happened from their windows.

"Just keep calm," said Kollberg. "There's no
danger."

He thought about this statement and laughed hol-
lowly.

"No, now the police are here," said Gunvald Larsson
over his shoulder.

The elevator was stopped about six floors up. The
door was open on the floor above and they could look
down the shaft. The elevator looked to be highly unus-
able. Someone had intentionally put it out of action. This
someone was in all probability the man on the roof. So
now they knew something else about him. He was a

good shot, he recognized them, and he knew something about elevators.

Always something, Kollberg thought.

Another flight up they were stopped by an iron door. It was locked and closed and probably barred and blocked from the other side, just how was hard to say.

On the other hand they could immediately determine that it couldn't be opened by ordinary means.

Gunvald Larsson wrinkled his bushy blond eyebrows.

"No point trying to beat it down," said Kollberg. "It won't help."

"We can kick in the door to one of the apartments down here," said Gunvald Larsson. "Then we can go out a window and try to get up that way."

"Without lines or ladders?"

"Right," said Gunvald Larsson. "It won't work."

He thought for a few seconds and went on.

"And what would you do on the roof? Without a pistol?"

Kollberg didn't answer.

"Of course it'll be the same story in the other entry," said Gunvald Larsson sourly.

It was the same story in the other entry, with the exception of an officious older man who claimed to be a retired army captain and who was holding the few people there under strict supervision.

"I was thinking of letting all the civilians take shelter in the basement," he said.

"Splendid," said Gunvald Larsson. "That's just what we'll do, Captain."

Otherwise it was a dismal repetition. Closed iron door, open elevator door and ruined elevator machinery. Chances of getting anywhere: zero.

Gunvald Larsson scratched himself thoughtfully on the chin with the barrel of his pistol.

Kollberg looked at the weapon nervously. A fine pistol, polished and well-cared-for, with a fluted walnut grip. The safety was on. He had never noticed a penchant for unnecessary gunfire among Gunvald Larsson's many reprehensible qualities.

"Have you ever shot anyone?" he asked suddenly.

"No. Why do you ask?"

"I don't know."

"I have a feeling we ought to get over to Odenplan," said Kollberg.

"Maybe so."

"We're the only ones with any real knowledge of the situation. At least we know what's happened."

It was evident that this suggestion didn't appeal to Gunvald Larsson. He jerked a hair from his left nostril and examined it absentmindedly.

"I'd like to get this character down off the roof," he said.

"But we can't get up there."

"No, we can't."

They went back down to the bottom floor. Just as they were about to leave the building they heard four shots.

"What's he shooting at now?" said Kollberg.

"The patrol car," said Gunvald Larsson. "He's practicing."

Kollberg looked at the empty patrol car and saw that both blue blinkers and the searchlight on the roof had been shot to pieces.

They left the building, keeping tightly to the wall and turned immediately to the left on Observatoriegatan. There wasn't a person in sight.

As soon as they'd rounded the corner they dropped their white coats on the sidewalk.

They heard a helicopter overhead, but they couldn't see it.

The wind had risen a bit and it was biting cold, despite the deceptive sunshine.

"Did you get the names of whoever lived up there?" asked Gunvald Larsson.

Kollberg nodded.

"Apparently there are two penthouse apartments, but one of them seems to be vacant."

"And the other one?"

"Somebody named Eriksson. A man and his daughter, as I understand it."

"Check."

In summary: someone who was a good shot, had access to an automatic weapon, recognized Kollberg and Gunvald Larsson, didn't like policemen, knew something about elevators, and might be named Eriksson.

They walked swiftly.

Sirens were wailing in the distance and nearby.

"We'll probably have to take him from outside," Kollberg said.

Gunvald Larsson didn't seem convinced.

"Maybe," he said.

If there were no people to be seen on Dalagatan or in its immediate vicinity, there were all the more in Odenplan. The triangular square was literally swarming with black-and-white cars and uniformed policemen and, not surprisingly, this massive deployment had drawn a large audience. The roadblocks so hastily thrown up had produced chaos in the traffic. The effects were in fact visible all through central Stockholm, but right here they were most spectacular. Odengatan was jammed with standing vehicles all the way to Valhallavägen, a score of busses were stuck fast in the muddle on the square itself, and all the empty taxicabs already in the square when the confusion began didn't make matters any better. To a man, the drivers had abandoned their taxis and were mingling with the police and the crowd.

Everyone wondering what it was all about.

More and more people arrived steadily from every direction, but especially up out of the subway. A mass of motorcycle policemen, two fire trucks and a traffic surveillance helicopter completed the picture. Here and there were groups of uniformed police, trying to obtain elbow room under baffling circumstances.

It couldn't have looked worse if the late Nyman had been directing it all himself, thought Kollberg, as he and Gunvald Larsson pushed their way toward the subway entrance, which seemed to mark the focus of activity.

And where they also found a man it might be useful to talk to, namely, Hansson of the Fifth Precinct. Or rather Lieutenant Norman Hansson, an Adolf Fredrik veteran who really knew his precinct inside out.

"Are you running this show?" Kollberg asked him.

"Good God, no."

Hansson looked around in alarm.

"Who is then?"

"There seem to be quite a few candidates, but Superintendent Malm just got here. He's in the van over there."

They pushed their way over to the van.

Malm was a trim, elegant man in his fifties, with a pleasant smile and curly hair. Rumor had it he stayed in condition by horseback riding on Djurgården. His political reliability was above all suspicion and on paper his credentials were superb. But his qualifications as a policeman were more open to question—indeed there were those who questioned their very existence.

"Good heavens, Larsson, you look terrible," he said.

"Where's Beck?" Kollberg asked.

"I haven't been in touch with him. And anyway, this is a case for specialists."

"What specialists?"

"From the regular police, of course," said Malm irritably. "Now it turns out the Commissioner is out of town and the Chief of the Metropolitan Police is on leave. But I've been in touch with the National Chief. He's out in Stocksund, and . . ."

"Splendid," said Gunvald Larsson.

"What do you mean by that?" said Malm suspiciously.

"That he's out of range," said Gunvald Larsson innocently.

"What? Well, in any case I've been given this command. I understand you've just come from the scene. How do you assess the situation?"

"There's some crazy son of a bitch sitting on a roof with an automatic rifle shooting policemen," said Gunvald Larsson.

Malm looked at him expectantly, but nothing else was forthcoming.

Gunvald Larsson beat his arms against his sides to keep warm.

"He's well entrenched from the inside," Kollberg said. "And the surrounding roofs are lower. Part of the time he's in an apartment up there, what's more. So far we haven't had a glimpse of him. In other words, it may be hard to get at him."

"Oh yes, there are lots of ways," said Malm loftily. "We're the ones with the resources."

Kollberg turned to Hansson.

"What happened to that car that got shot up on Odengatan?"

"Too much," said Hansson sullenly. "Two men wounded, one in the arm and one in the leg. May I make a suggestion?"

"What?" said Gunvald Larsson.

"That we move away from here. To someplace inside the cordon, for example the gas works lot on Torsgatan."

"Where the old gasholder was," said Kollberg.

"Right. They tore it down. They're going to build a cloverleaf."

Kollberg sighed. The old brick gasholder had been a unique piece of architecture, and a few people with foresight had mounted a campaign to save it. Unsuccessfully, of course. Could anything be more important than a cloverleaf?

Kollberg shook himself. Why was he always thinking of things that were irrelevant? He was definitely getting a little dotty.

"Can the helicopters land there?" Malm asked.

"Yes."

"Malm threw a look at Gunvald Larsson.

"Is it . . . out of range?"

"Yes. Unless the bastard's got a mortar."

Malm paused for quite a while. Then he looked at his colleagues and made his announcement in a loud, clear voice.

"Gentlemen. I have an idea. We will move individually to the gas works area on Torsgatan. Regrouping there . . ."

He looked at his watch.

"In ten minutes."

27.

By the time Martin Beck and Rönn got to Torsgatan it was one thirty P.M. and everything seemed to be pretty well organized.

Malm had established himself in the old gatehouse at the west entrance to the hospital, and he was surrounded not only by considerable material resources but also by most of the policemen who had so far played significant roles in the drama. Even Hult was there, and Martin Beck walked straight over to him.

"I've been looking for you."

"Oh? What for?"

"It doesn't matter any more. It was just that Åke Eriksson used your name when he called the Nymans' last night."

"Åke Eriksson?"

"Yes."

"Åke Reinhold Eriksson?"

"Yes."

"Is he the one who murdered Stig Nyman?"

"So it seems."

"And who's sitting up there right now?"

"Yes. Probably."

Hult said nothing more and his face was expressionless, but he clenched his meaty red fists so the knuckles stood out like bone-white spots beneath the skin.

As far as anyone knew, the man on the roof hadn't made a move since taking target practice on the abandoned patrol car an hour before.

Despite the fact that they were now studying the building through field glasses, no one actually knew if he was even still alive. And so far the police hadn't fired a single shot.

"But the net is closing," said Malm, looking pleased.

This cliché was so moth-eaten that no one even had the strength to smile inwardly. What's more, for once it gave a fairly accurate picture of the situation.

Police had infiltrated the entire block the apartment house stood in. Most of them were equipped with walkie-talkies and could maintain contact with each other and with the mobile radio control parked outside the old hospital gate. There were tear-gas experts in the attics of the nearest buildings, and sharpshooters lay ready at what were considered important strategic points.

"There are only two such points," said Gunvald Larsson. "The roof of the Bonnier Building and the cupola of Gustav Vasa Church. Do you think the minister will let us send a sniper up in his steeple?"

No one was really listening to him.

The immediate plan had been determined. First, the man on the roof would be given a chance to surrender. Failing that, he would be taken by force, or shot. No more policemen's lives were to be risked. The decisive action would be taken from outside the building.

Hook-and-ladder trucks stood waiting on Observatoriegatan and Odengatan, ready to go into action if the situation seemed to demand it. They were manned by firemen, since someone had to operate the machinery, but also by policemen in firemen's uniforms.

Martin Beck and Rönn were able to contribute some important information. Namely that Eriksson—if it was Eriksson, that reservation still had to be made—was armed with an American-made Johnson automatic rifle and an ordinary army model semi-automatic rifle, both of them probably equipped with telescopic sights. Also with a target pistol, type Hammerli.

"Johnson automatic," said Gunvald Larsson. "Jesus Christ. It weighs less than fifteen pounds and it's exceptionally easy to handle and it's as good as a machine gun. Has a short recoil and raps out a hundred and sixty rounds a minute."

The only one listening was Rönn, who grunted thoughtful assent.

Then he yawned. No one got the better of nature.

"And with the Mauser he can hit a louse on a visiting card at six hundred meters. With good visibility and a little luck he could hit a man at over a thousand."

Kollberg, who was leaning over a map of the city, nodded.

"Imagine what he can do just to amuse himself," said Gunvald Larsson.

Gunvald Larsson had been amusing himself by working out ranges. From the roof where he'd entrenched himself, Eriksson lay 150 meters from the intersection of Odengatan and Hälsingegatan, 250 from the central hospital at Mount Sabbath, 300 from Gustav Vasa Church, 500 meters from the Bonnier Building, 1,000 from the first skyscraper at Hötorget, and 1,100 from the City Hall.

Malm waved away these observations patronizingly and irritably.

"Yes, yes," he said. "Don't worry about that now."

The only one who wasn't thinking much about teargas bombs and helicopters, water cannon and walkie-talkies was Martin Beck.

He was standing quietly in a corner, and not just because of his usual claustrophobia and aversion to crowds. He was thinking about Ake Eriksson and the circumstances that had driven the man into the absurd and desperate situation in which he now obviously found himself. It was possible that Eriksson's mind was now completely in eclipse, that he was beyond communication and human contact, but it wasn't certain. Someone was responsible for all of this. Not Nyman, because he had never understood what responsibility for human beings actually meant, or even that such an idea existed. Not Malm of course, for whom Eriksson was quite simply a dangerous madman on a roof, with no other connection to the police than that it was their job, one way or another, to put him out of action.

And Martin Beck felt something growing stronger and stronger in his mind. A sense of guilt, a guilt he might actively have to come to terms with.

Ten minutes later, the man on the roof shot a patrolman standing on the corner of Odengatan and Torsgatan, five hundred meters from the window from which the shot had clearly been fired. The surprising thing was not so much the distance as the fact that he'd been able to get a clear shot through all the leafless branches in the park.

However it happened, the shot went home, striking the patrolman in the shoulder. Since he was wearing a bulletproof vest, the wound was not too serious, at least not critical.

Eriksson fired just that one shot—maybe it was some kind of a show of strength, or a purely reflex action. A demonstration of the fact that he shot at policemen wherever he could find them.

"Is it possible he's got the little girl up there with him?" Kollberg asked suddenly. "As a hostage?"

Rönn shook his head.

The child was in good hands, out of danger.

Out of danger from her father? Had she ever been in danger in his presence?

A little while later everything was ready for the crucial assault.

Malm inspected the specially trained policemen who were to carry out the capture itself. Or liquidation, if that proved to be necessary. In all probability it would prove to be necessary. No one seriously believed that the man on the roof would simply surrender. But of course the possibility existed. Many similar situations in criminal history had ended with the desperado—the universally accepted term for persons of Eriksson's type— suddenly growing tired of the whole affair and giving himself up to superior force.

The specialists who were to put an end to the terror —the same old well-worn expressions cropped up again and again, there didn't seem to be any others—were two young policemen with comprehensive training in hand-to-hand combat and surprise attack.

Martin Beck also went out and talked to them.

One of them was a redhead named Lenn Axelsson. His smile had a sort of hard-won self-assurance that was very likable. The other was blonder and more serious but inspired equal confidence. Both were volunteers, though the special branch of the force they represented took it for granted that even difficult assignments would be executed promptly and voluntarily.

They both seemed clever and pleasant, and their faith in their own ability was infectious. Good, dependable men, with first-rate training. The department had no great abundance of such men—capable, brave, and far more intelligent than average. Thanks to both theoretical and practical instruction, they were well acquainted with what was expected of them. It seemed somehow that the whole exercise would go off smoothly and easily. These boys knew their special job and were very sure of themselves. Axelsson joked and even told and laughed at a story of how, as a cadet, he had approached Martin Beck with a show of camaraderie, and less than the most fortunate results. Martin Beck couldn't remember the incident at all, but to be on the safe side he laughed anyway, if somewhat weakly.

The two men were well equipped, with bulletproof vests as well as bulletproof breeches. Steel helmets with plexiglass visors, gas masks and, as their primary armament, light, effective automatic weapons of the kind called machine-pistols in Sweden. They also carried tear-gas grenades for all eventualities, and their physical training guaranteed that in case of hand-to-hand combat, either one of them could easily overpower a person like Åke Eriksson.

The plan of attack was seductively simple and direct. The man on the roof was first to be put out of action by a concentrated rain of tear-gas cartridges and grenades, then the helicopters would fly in low and set down the two police commandos on either side of the criminal. He would be taken from two directions and, already incapacitated by gas, his chances should be minimal.

Only Gunvald Larsson seemed opposed to the plan, but he couldn't manage or wouldn't take the trouble to state any objection other than that, in spite of everything, he still preferred the idea of trying to get at Eriksson from inside the building.

"We're going to do this the way I say," said Malm. "I don't want any more risky schemes and personal heroics. These boys have been trained for situations like this. We know they've got a ninety percent chance of succeeding. And the prospects of at least one of them making it completely uninjured are just about one hundred percent. So no more amateurish objections. Understood?"

"Understood," said Gunvald Larsson. "Heil Hitler!"

Malm jumped as if someone had run him through with a red-hot poker.

"I won't forget that," he said. "You can count on it."

Everyone in hearing looked at Gunvald Larsson reproachfully. Even Rönn, who was standing beside him.

"That was a hell of a dumb thing to say, Gunvald," he said under his breath.

"Says you," said Gunvald Larsson dryly.

So the final phase began, calmly and systematically. An amplifier truck was driven up through the hospital grounds to almost in sight of the roof. But only almost. The speaker horn was aimed, and Malm's voice thundered up toward the besieged building. He said exactly what everyone had a right to expect him to say.

"Attention, please! This is Superintendent Malm. I don't know you, Mr. Eriksson, and you don't know me. But I can give you my word as a professional that it's all over. You're surrounded, and our resources are unlimited. But we don't want to use more force than the situation demands, especially considering all the innocent women and children and other civilians who are still in the danger area. You've already caused enough, more than enough suffering, Eriksson. You now have ten minutes in which to surrender of your own free will. Like a man of honor. I beg you, for your own sake, show some compassion, and accept the compassion we offer you now."

It sounded fine.

But there was no answer. Not even a shot.

"I wonder if he's acted in anticipation of events," Malm said to Martin Beck.

Yes, the language really was impoverished.

Exactly ten minutes later the helicopters took off.

They whirled out in wide arcs, at first quite high, and then moved in toward the roof with its small balconies and two penthouse apartments. From two directions.

At the same time, tear-gas projectiles began to rain

down on the building from every side. A few of them
broke windows and exploded inside, but most of them
landed on the roof and the balconies.

Gunvald Larsson was in perhaps the best position to
follow the events of the final phase. He had gone up to
the roof of the Bonnier Building and was lying behind
the parapet. When the tear-gas bombs started popping
and the sickly clouds of gas began spreading out across
the roof, he stood up and put his field glasses to his
eyes.

The helicopters carried out their pincer movement
impeccably. The one from the south arrived a little before the other, but that was according to plan.

Now it was already hovering over the south part of
the roof. The plexiglass bubble opened and the crew
started lowering the commando on a line. It was the
redhead, Axelsson, and he looked formidable in his bulletproof clothing, his machine gun grasped firmly in
both hands. Gas grenades hooked to his belt.

Two feet from the ground he lifted his face guard and
started putting on his gas mask. He came closer and
closer to the roof, the machine gun at the ready in the
crook of his right arm.

And now Eriksson, if that's who it was, should come
stumbling out of the cloud of gas and throw down his
weapons.

When likable, red-haired Axelsson was six inches
from the roof, a single shot was fired. Bulletproof clothing may be all very well, but it can never protect the entire face.

In spite of the distance, Gunvald Larsson could see
all the details. The body, which gave a start and went
limp, even the bullet hole between the eyes.

The helicopter leaped upward, paused for several
seconds, then swept across the tops of the buildings and
in over the hospital complex, with the dead policeman
dangling on a line from the body of the ship. The machine gun was still hanging on its sling, and the dead
man's arms and legs swayed limply in the wind.

He had never got the gas mask more than halfway
on.

For the first time, Gunvald Larsson now caught a

glimpse of the man on the roof. A tall figure in some kind of an overall shifted position quickly not far from the chimney. He couldn't spot any weapon, but he saw clearly that the man was wearing a gas mask.

The second helicopter had broken off its part of the pincer movement from the north and now hovered motionless several yards above the roof, the door in its plexiglass bubble already open, stormtrooper number two ready to descend.

And then came the fusillade. The man on the roof had gone back to his Johnson automatic and in less than a minute fired off at least a hundred rounds. The shots could not be seen, but the range was so short that almost all of them must have struck.

The helicopter swept away toward Vasa Park, wobbled, and lost altitude. Missed the top of the Eastman Institute by inches, tried with a roar to right itself, slipped sideways and crashed thunderously in the middle of the park, where it lay on its side like a shot-gunned crow.

The first helicopter was already back at the takeoff point with a dead policeman swinging between its landing gear. It came down on the gas works lot. Axelsson's body bounced on the ground and was dragged for several yards.

The rotors stopped.

Then came the impotent substitute for revenge. Hundreds of different weapons belched out bullets toward the building on Dalagatan. Few of them with any definite target, and none of them with any effect.

The police opened fire, futilely, but presumably to regain their courage. Shots were fired from hopeless angles and impossible ranges.

No shots were fired from the Bonnier Building or from Gustav Vasa Church.

It took several minutes for the gunfire to die down and stop.

That anyone might have hit Åke Eriksson (if in fact that's who it was) seemed utterly out of the question.

28.

The temporary headquarters was an exceptionally cute little yellow wooden house with a black metal roof, an enclosed porch, and a tall hood on the chimney.

Twenty minutes after the unsuccessful airborne landing, most of the assembly were still in shock.

"He shot down the helicopter," said Malm in disbelief and probably for the tenth time.

"Oh, so you've come to that conclusion too," said Gunvald Larsson, who had just returned from his observation post.

"I'll have to ask for military assistance," said Malm.

"Oh I don't think . . ." said Kollberg.

"Yes," said Malm. "That's our only chance."

The only chance to dump the responsibility on someone else without too great a loss of prestige, thought Kollberg. What could the army do?

"What can the army do?" said Martin Beck.

"Bomb the building," said Gunvald Larsson. "Barrage this part of town with artillery. Or . . ."

Martin Beck looked at him.

"Or what?"

"Call in the paratroops. Might not even have to use people. We could drop a dozen police dogs."

"Sarcasm is extremely out of place at this particular moment," said Martin Beck.

Gunvald Larsson didn't reply. Rönn suddenly spoke up instead. For some reason he had chosen this moment to study his notes.

"Well, I see this happens to be Eriksson's thirty-sixth birthday."

"Hell of a funny way to celebrate," said Gunvald Larsson. "But wait a minute. If we set up the police orchestra on the street and play 'Happy Birthday to You,' that might put him in a jolly mood. And then we could drop him a poison birthday cake with thirty-six candles."

"Shut up, Gunvald," said Martin Beck.

"We haven't used the fire department," said Malm.

"No," said Kollberg. "But after all it wasn't the fire department that killed his wife. He's got damned good vision, and as soon as it dawns on him that there are disguised policemen among the firemen . . ."

He stopped.

"What does Eriksson's wife have to do with this?" Malm asked.

"A good deal," said Kollberg.

"Oh, that old story," said Malm. "But there is something to what you say. Maybe some relative could talk him into giving up. His girl friend, for example."

"He doesn't have one," Rönn said.

"Okay, but anyway. Maybe his daughter or his parents."

Kollberg shivered. It seemed more and more evident that the Superintendent had picked up his knowledge of police work at the movies.

Malm got up and walked out to the cars.

Kollberg looked long and searchingly at Martin Beck. But Martin Beck didn't meet his gaze. He was standing by the wall in the old gate-keeper's room and looked somehow sad and inaccessible.

Nor did the situation warrant any particular optimism.

There were now three people dead—Nyman, Kvant and Axelsson—and with the crash of the helicopter, the number of injured had risen to seven. Those were sinister statistics. Kollberg hadn't had time to feel anything in particular while he was trying to save his own life outside the Eastman Institute, but now he was afraid. Afraid, partly, that further recklessness would cost the lives of still more policemen, but mostly that Eriksson would suddenly abandon the principle of shooting only at the police. Because at that instant the scope of the disaster would expand enormously. There were all too many people within his range, most of them in the hospital complex or in the apartments along Odengatan. And what could anyone do about it? If time really counted, there was only one way out. To somehow storm the roof. And what would that cost?

Kollberg wondered what Martin Beck was thinking. He wasn't used to being left in the dark on that point, and it irritated him to be so now. But it didn't last long, because just then the Superintendent appeared in the doorway, and Martin Beck looked up at him.

"This is a one-man job," he said.

"For who?"

"For me."

"I can't permit that," said Malm at once.

"If you'll excuse me, it's my decision to make."

"Just a minute," said Kollberg. "What are you basing that conclusion on? Technical considerations? Or moral ones?"

Martin Beck looked at him but said nothing.

For Kollberg that was answer enough. Both.

And if Martin Beck had made the decision, Kollberg wasn't the man to oppose it. They knew each other too well for that, and too long.

"How are you planning to do it?" said Gunvald Larsson.

"Get into one of the apartments below him and go out through a window toward the yard. The window under the balcony on the north. And go up with a grappling ladder."

"Yes, that might work," said Gunvald Larsson.

"Where do you want Eriksson?" Kollberg asked.

"Toward the street, and preferably on the upper roof, on top of the north penthouse."

Kollberg wrinkled his forehead and put his left thumb against his upper lip.

"He probably won't go there willingly," said Gunvald Larsson. "Because he'd be vulnerable there. For a good shot."

"Wait a minute," Kollberg said. "If I've got the construction of the roof straight, the penthouses sit on the actual roof of the building like boxes. They're a couple of yards in from the street, and between the penthouse roofs and the outer edge there's a slanting glass roof that slopes in. So there's a hollow there."

Martin Beck looked at him.

"Yes, that's right," Kollberg went on, "and I have the

feeling he was lying right there when he shot at the car on Odengatan."

"But at that point he wasn't running the risk of getting shot at himself," Gunvald Larsson objected. "But by this time a sharpshooter on top of the Bonnier Building or up in the church tower . . . no, wait, I guess not from the Bonnier Building."

"And he hasn't thought of the church tower," Kollberg said. "For that matter, there isn't anyone up there anyway."

"No," said Gunvald Larsson. "Stupidly enough."

"Okay. Now to get him over there, or at least to get him up on the penthouse roof, we'll have to do something to draw his attention."

Kollberg furrowed his brow again and everyone else was quiet.

"That building is a little farther from the street than the ones on either side," he said. "Roughly six feet. I figure if we do something right down in the corner, in the angle where the two buildings come together, and as close to them as possible, he'll have to get up on the upper roof in order to see. He'd hardly dare just lean out over the rail on the lower level. We could have one of the fire trucks . . ."

"I don't want any firemen involved," said Martin Beck.

"We can use the police that are already in firemen's uniforms. And if they stick close to the walls he can hardly get at them."

"Unless he's got some hand grenades," said Gunvald Larsson pessimistically.

"And what will they do?" asked Martin Beck.

"Make noise," Kollberg said. "That's enough. I'll take care of that detail. But you, on the other hand, you've got to be quiet as hell."

Martin Beck nodded.

"Yes," said Kollberg. "I guess you know that."

Malm looked narrowly at Martin Beck.

"Am I to regard you as a volunteer?" he asked finally.

"Yes."

"I have to say I admire you," said Malm. "But frankly I don't understand you."

Martin Beck didn't answer.

He entered the building on Dalagatan fifteen minutes later. He'd stuck close to the walls, with the interlinking light metal ladders under his arm.

At the same time, one of the fire trucks, siren wailing, swung around the corner from Observatoriegatan.

He was carrying the little shortwave radio in his coat pocket and his 7.65 mm Walther in its shoulder holster. He waved off one of the civilian-clad patrolmen who'd sneaked in by way of the furnace room and started slowly up the stairs.

When he reached the top he opened the apartment door with a master key that Kollberg had somehow produced, went in, hung his overcoat and jacket in the hall.

He automatically glanced around at the apartment, which was tastefully and pleasantly furnished, and wondered for a moment who lived there.

The deafening bellow of the fire engine went on through it all.

Martin Beck felt calm and relaxed. He opened the window at the back of the building and took his bearings. He was directly under the north balcony. He assembled the ladder, threaded it out through the window and hooked it fast to the rail of the balcony ten feet farther up.

Then he stepped down from the window, walked back into the apartment and switched on his radio. He made contact with Rönn at once.

From his point on top of the Bonnier Building, five hundred yards to the southwest and over twenty stories above the ground, Einar Rönn stared across the hospital complex toward the building on Dalagatan. There were tears in his eyes from the fresh wind, but he could quite distinctly see the spot he was supposed to observe. The roof of the penthouse on the north.

"Nothing," he said into the radio. "Still nothing."

He heard the fire engine howling, and then he saw a shadow slither across the little sunlit piece of roof and he put his mouth to the radio.

"Yes. Now," he said, rather excitedly. "Now he's up there. On this side. He's lying down."

Twenty-five seconds later the siren stopped. For Rönn, half a kilometer away, the difference was slight. But only an instant later he again saw the patch of shadow on the roof over there far away, and he saw a figure rise to his feet and he said, "Martin! Come in!"

This time his voice was really excited. No one answered.

If Rönn had been a good shot, which he wasn't, and if he'd had a rifle with a telescopic sight, which he didn't, he would have had a chance of hitting the figure on the roof. If he'd had the nerve to shoot, which he doubted. By this time, the person he saw might actually be Martin Beck.

For Einar Rönn, it didn't mean much that a fuse blew in the fire truck and the scream of the siren stopped.

For Martin Beck, it meant everything.

As soon as he got Rönn's signal he put down the radio, twisted out through the window and climbed quickly up to the balcony. Directly in front of him he had the windowless rear of the penthouse and a narrow, rusty iron ladder.

When the protecting siren was cut off, he found himself on the way up this ladder with his pistol in his right hand.

In the wake of the massive, vibrating howl came what seemed like total silence.

The barrel of his pistol hit the right side of the iron ladder with a light echoing clang.

Martin Beck heaved himself up to the roof, had his head and shoulders already over the edge.

Six feet in front of him stood Ake Eriksson, his feet set wide on the roof, his target pistol aimed straight at Martin Beck's chest.

He himself was still holding his Walther pointed up and to one side, caught in the middle of a movement.

What did he have time to think?

That it was too late.

That he recognized Eriksson more readily than he'd

expected to—the blond mustache, the combed-back hair. The gas mask pushed around to the back of his neck.

That's what he had time to see. Plus the oddly shaped Hammerli with its huge grip and the steel-blue material of the square barrel. The pistol staring at him with death's small black eye.

He'd read that somewhere.

Most of all, that it was too late.

Eriksson shot. He saw the blue eyes just in that hundredth of a second.

And the flash from the muzzle.

The bullet struck him in the middle of the chest. Like a sledgehammer.

29.

The little balcony was roughly six feet deep and ten feet long. A narrow iron ladder was firmly bolted to the inside wall, and led up to the black sheet-iron roof. On the two short walls there were closed doors into the building, while on the side toward the yard was a high railing of thick opaque glass plates, and above it an iron beam that ran between the outside corners of the two side walls. On the glazed brick tiles of the balcony floor stood a collapsible rack for beating carpets.

Martin Beck lay on his back on this sparse network of galvanized iron pipes. His head was bent back and his neck rested against the heavy pipe that constituted the frame of the carpet rack.

He slowly regained consciousness, opened his eyes and looked up into the clear blue sky. His vision began to swim and he closed his eyes again.

He remembered, or rather perhaps still felt, the terrible impact against his chest and how he had fallen. But he had no memory of landing. Had he plunged down into the yard, the whole height of the building? Could a man survive a fall like that?

Martin Beck tried to lift his head to look around, but

when he tensed his muscles the pain was so piercing that for a moment he passed out again. He didn't repeat the attempt, but looked around from under half-closed lids as well as he could without moving his head. He could see the ladder and the black edge of the roof, and realized that his fall hadn't been more than a couple of yards.

He closed his eyes. Then he tried to move his arms and legs one at a time, but the pain stabbed at him as soon as he moved a muscle anywhere. He realized he'd been hit by at least one shot in the chest, and he was mildly surprised to be alive. He was not, however, gripped by the dizzying joy that the people in novels seemed to feel in these situations. Nor, oddly enough, was he afraid.

He wondered how much time had passed since he'd been hit, and whether he'd been hit again after losing consciousness. Was the man still up there on the roof? He didn't hear any shots.

Martin Beck had seen his face, at once the face of a child and of an old man. How was that possible? And his eyes—insane with fear or hate or desperation, or maybe just utterly vacant.

Martin Beck had somehow imagined that he understood this man, that a part of the fault was his own, that he must help, but the man on the roof was beyond all help. At some point during the last twenty-four hours he had taken the decisive step across the border into insanity, into a world where nothing existed except revenge, violence and hate.

Now I'm lying here and maybe dying, thought Martin Beck, and what kind of guilt do I atone for by dying?

None at all.

He was frightened by his own thoughts and it suddenly seemed to him he'd been lying there motionless for an eternity. Had the man on the roof been killed or captured, was it all over and he had been forgotten, left to die, alone, on a little balcony?

Martin Beck tried to shout, but all that came out was a gurgling sound and he tasted blood in his mouth.

He lay completely still and wondered where the powerful roaring noise came from. It was all around him and sounded like strong wind in the tops of trees or like breakers on an ocean beach, or was it maybe coming from some air-conditioning machinery somewhere nearby?

Martin Beck felt himself sinking in a soft, silent darkness where the roar died away, and he didn't bother to fight it. He came back to the roar and shimmering phosphorescent flashes in the blood-red light behind his eyelids, and before he sank again he realized that the rushing sound was somewhere inside himself.

His consciousness left him and came back and left him and came back, as if he were being rocked on a heavy, listless swell, and through his brain passed visions and fragments of thought he no longer had the strength to grasp. He heard mumbling and distant sounds and voices from inside the growing roar, but nothing concerned him any more.

He was plunging down into a thundering shaft of darkness.

30.

Kollberg rapped his shortwave radio nervously with his knuckles.

"What happened?"

The radio gave a short burst of static, but for the moment that was all.

"What happened?" he repeated.

Gunvald Larsson walked up to him with long strides.

"To the fire engine? They had a short circuit."

"I don't mean the fire engine," said Kollberg. "What happened to Martin? Yes, hello? Hello? Come in."

It crackled again, a little louder this time, and then Rönn's voice came through, vague and uncertain.

"What happened?" it said.

"I don't know," Kollberg shouted. "What can you see?"

"Nothing right now."

"What did you see before?"

"Hard to say. I think I saw Eriksson. He came out to the edge of the roof, and I gave Martin the signal. Then . . ."

"Yes?" Kollberg said impatiently. "Hurry up."

"Well, then the siren stopped and right afterward Eriksson stood up. I think so anyway. He stood straight up, with his back toward me."

"Did you see Martin?"

"No, not once."

"And now?"

"Nothing at all," Rönn said. "There's no one there."

"Fuck!" said Kollberg and dropped the hand with the walkie-talkie.

Gunvald Larsson grunted unhappily.

They were standing on Observatoriegatan, quite close to the corner of Dalagatan and less than a hundred yards from the building. Malm was there too, and a lot of other people with him.

A fire department officer walked up to them.

"You want the hook-and-ladder to stay out there?"

Malm looked at Kollberg and Gunvald Larsson. He no longer seemed quite so eager to give orders.

"No," said Kollberg. "Have them drive it back. There's no point in their exposing themselves any longer than necessary."

"Well," said Gunvald Larsson. "It doesn't look like Beck made it, does it?"

"No," said Kollberg quietly. "It doesn't."

"Wait a minute," someone said. "Listen to this."

It was Norman Hansson. He said something into his radio, then he turned to Kollberg.

"I've got a man up in the church tower now. He thinks maybe he sees Beck."

"Yes? Where?"

"He's lying on the north balcony toward the yard."

Hansson looked at Kollberg gravely.

"He seems to be injured."

"Injured? Is he moving?"

"Not now. But my man thinks he saw him move a couple minutes ago."

This observation might be accurate. Rönn couldn't see the back of the building from Bonnier's. But the church was to the north, and two hundred yards closer, what's more.

"We have to get him down from there," Kollberg muttered.

"We have to put an end to this whole spectacle," said Gunvald Larsson gloomily.

"For that matter," he went on, a few seconds later, "it was a mistake to go up there alone. One hell of a mistake."

"Keep your peace in front of men and slander them behind their backs," Kollberg said. "Do you know what that is, Larsson?"

Gunvald Larsson looked at him for a long time.

"This isn't Moscow or Peking," he said then, with unusual severity. "The cabbies don't read Gorky here, and the cops don't quote Lenin. This is an insane city in a country that's mentally deranged. And up there on the roof there's some poor damned lunatic and now it's time to bring him down."

"Quite right," said Kollberg. "For that matter, it wasn't Lenin."

"I know."

"What the hell are you talking about?" said Malm nervously.

Neither of them even looked at him.

"Okay," said Gunvald Larsson. "You go get your buddy Beck, and I'll take care of the other one."

Kollberg nodded.

He turned to walk over to the firemen but then stopped himself.

"Do you know what I figure your chances are of getting off that roof alive? By your method?"

"Roughly," said Gunvald Larsson.

Then he looked at the people standing around him.

"I'm going to blow the door and storm the roof from the inside," he said in a loud voice. "I'll need one man to help me. Two at the most."

Four or five young policemen and a fireman raised their hands, and right behind him a voice said, "Take me."

"Don't misunderstand me now," said Gunvald Larsson. "I don't want anyone who thinks it's his duty, and no one who thinks he's great stuff and wants to impress everybody. The chances of getting killed are better than any of you dream."

"What do you mean?" said Malm bewilderedly. "Who do you want then?"

"The only ones I'm interested in are the ones who really want to take a chance at getting shot. Who think it's fun."

"Take me."

Gunvald Larsson turned around and looked at the man who'd spoken.

"Yes, you," he said. "Hult. Yes, that's fine. I guess you'd like to go all right."

"Hey, here," said one of the men on the sidewalk. "I'd like to go."

A slim blond man in his thirties, wearing jeans and a leather jacket.

"Who are you?"

"Name's Bohlin."

"Are you even a policeman?"

"No, I'm a construction worker."

"How did you get here?"

"I live here."

Gunvald Larsson examined him thoughtfully.

"Okay," he said. "Give him a pistol."

Norman Hansson immediately took out his service automatic, which he was carrying quite simply in the breast pocket of his coat, but Bohlin didn't want it."

"Can I use my own?" he said. "It'll only take a minute to get it."

Gunvald Larsson nodded. The man left.

"That's actually illegal," said Malm. "It's . . . wrong."

"Yes," said Gunvald Larsson. "It's wrong as all hell. Most of all that there's anyone with a gun to volunteer."

Bohlin was back in less than a minute with the gun in his hand. A .22 Colt Huntsman, with a long barrel and ten rounds in the magazine.

"Well, let's get going then," said Gunvald Larsson.

He paused and looked at Kollberg, who was already on his way around the corner with two long coils of rope on his arm.

"We'll let Kollberg go up first and bring down Beck," he went on. "Hansson, get some men to drill and set the charges in the doors."

Hansson nodded and walked away.

A little while later they were ready.

"Okay," said Gunvald Larsson.

He walked around the corner, followed by the other two.

"You take the south entrance," he said when they got to the building. "I'll take the north. When you've lit the fuse, run down at least one flight. Preferably two. Can you make it, Hult?"

"Yes."

"Good. And one more thing. If either of you kills him up there, then whoever does it will have to answer for it later."

"Even if it's in self-defense?" Hult asked.

"Right. Even if it's in self-defense. Now let's synchronize our watches."

Lennart Kollberg turned the handle to the apartment. The door was locked, but he already had a passkey in his hand and quickly opened it. He noticed Martin Beck's coat on a hanger and the shortwave radio on a table as he entered the front hall, and as soon as he went on into the apartment he saw the open window and the lower part of the metal ladder outside. It looked frail and fragile, and he'd gained a good many pounds since the last time he'd climbed such a ladder, but he knew it was built to support heavier bodies than his and he climbed up into the window without hesitating.

He made sure the two coils of rope, which were over his shoulders and crossed on his chest, wouldn't get in his way or catch on the ladder, and then he climbed slowly and carefully up to the balcony.

Ever since Rönn reported what he'd seen through his field glasses, Kollberg had been telling himself that the worst could have happened, and he thought he was prepared. But when he heaved himself up to climb over the railing and saw Martin Beck lying bloody and lifeless only three feet away, he gasped for breath.

He launched himself over the railing and leaned down over Martin Beck's pale yellow upturned face.

"Martin," he whispered hoarsely. "Martin, for God's sake . . ."

And as he said it he saw an artery working in Martin Beck's taut throat. Kollberg put his fingers carefully on the pulse. It was beating, but very sluggishly.

He checked over his friend's body. As far as he could tell, Martin Beck had been hit by only one shot, in the middle of his chest.

The bullet had made an amazingly small hole between the buttons. Kollberg ripped open the shirt, which was drenched with blood. To judge by the oval shape of the wound, the bullet had struck slightly from one side and continued on into the right half of the thorax. He couldn't determine if it had come out the other side or was still inside the chest.

He looked at the floor underneath the rack. A pool of blood had gathered, not particularly large, and the flow of blood from the wound had almost stopped.

Kollberg slipped the coils of rope over his head, hung one of them on the carpet rack's upper crossbar, then paused with the other in his hand and listened. There wasn't a sound from the roof. He unrolled the line and slipped one end carefully under Martin Beck's back. He handled the rope quickly and silently, and when he was done he checked to see that it lay around Martin Beck the way it should, and that the knots were properly tied. Finally he felt in Martin Beck's pockets, found a clean handkerchief, and took his own somewhat less clean one from his trousers pocket.

He took off his cashmere scarf, tied it around Martin Beck's chest and put the two folded handkerchiefs between the knot and the wound.

He still didn't hear a sound.

Now came the hard part.

Kollberg leaned over the balcony railing and looked down, then moved the ladder so it hung right beside the open window. Then he carefully slid the rack up to the railing, took the loose end of the rope he'd tied around Beck, wound it a couple of turns around the railing where the ladder had been, and knotted it around his own waist.

He lifted Martin Beck carefully over the edge while exerting a counter force with his own body so that the rope stayed taut. When Martin Beck was hanging free on the other side of the glass balustrade, Kollberg started loosening the knot at his waist with his right hand while he held the entire weight of the other man's body with his left. When he'd undone the knot he slowly started lowering Martin Beck. He held tightly with both hands and without looking over the rail tried to estimate how much line he needed to play out.

When, according to his calculations, Martin Beck ought to be hanging outside the open window, Kollberg leaned over to look. He let out a few more inches and tied the line firmly around the iron railing above the glass.

Then he picked up the other coil of rope from the carpet rack, put it over his shoulder, climbed quickly down the ladder and in through the window.

Apparently lifeless, Martin Beck hung a foot and a half below the window ledge. His head had fallen forward and his body was suspended slightly at an angle.

Kollberg made sure his footing was secure and leaned out over the windowsill. He grasped the line with both hands and started to haul. He shifted his grip to one hand, caught hold of the rope under Martin Beck's arms, lifted him up, grabbed him under the shoulders and dragged him through the window.

When he'd removed the rope and laid him on the floor, he climbed the ladder again, untied the rope from the railing and let it fall. When he was back in the window, he unhooked the ladder and brought it down.

Then he lifted Martin Beck onto his back and started down the stairs.

Gunvald Larsson had six seconds left when he discovered he'd committed what was probably the worst oversight of his career. He was standing in front of the iron door, looking at the fuse he was supposed to light, and he had no matches. Since he didn't smoke, a lighter wasn't part of his equipment. When, very rarely, he went out to the Riche or the Park he generally stuffed a couple books of their monogrammed matches in his pocket. But he'd changed coats countless times since the last time he'd been out to eat.

His jaw dropped, as the saying goes, and with his mouth still open in perplexity, he drew his pistol, took off the safety, held the muzzle against the end of the fuse—with the barrel aimed at an angle against the door so he wouldn't get a ricochet in some inconvenient place, his stomach for example—and pulled the trigger. The bullet whined around in the stone stairwell like a hornet, but in any case the fuse was lit, fizzing away with a merry blue flame, and he ran down the stairs. One and a half flights down, the house vibrated from the detonation in B-entry and then his own charge went off, four seconds late.

But he was faster than Hult, and probably faster than Bohlin too, and he made up one or two of those seconds in his rush up the stairs. The iron door had disappeared, or, that is, it was lying flat on the landing where it belonged, and half a flight farther up was a steel-reinforced glass door.

He kicked it down and found himself on the roof. To be exact, right next to the chimney between the two penthouse apartments.

He saw Eriksson at once, standing legs astraddle on the penthouse roof with the much discussed Johnson automatic in his hands. But Eriksson didn't see Gunvald Larsson. His interest was apparently completely occupied by the first explosion and his attention was directed to the south half of the building.

Gunvald Larsson put one foot on the guard rail toward the street, gathered his weight and landed on the penthouse roof. Eriksson turned his head and looked at him.

The distance between them was only twelve feet and the outcome was clear. Gunvald Larsson had the man in his sights and his finger on the trigger.

But Eriksson didn't seem to care. He went on turning, swinging the automatic around toward his antagonist. And Gunvald Larsson didn't shoot.

He stood motionlessly with his pistol aimed at Eriksson's chest, and the barrel of the rifle continued to swing.

Just then Bohlin fired. It was a masterful shot. His view was largely blocked by Gunvald Larsson, but with unerring precision he nevertheless put a bullet in Eriksson's left shoulder, from a range of more than sixty feet.

The automatic rifle rattled down onto the metal roof, and Eriksson twisted halfway around and sank down on all fours.

Then Hult was there, slamming the flat side of his pistol into the back of Eriksson's head. The blow made a cruel-sounding smack.

The man on the roof lay unconscious, with blood streaming from his head.

Hult was breathing hard. He lifted his weapon again.

"Hold it," said Gunvald Larsson. "That's plenty."

He put his own pistol back on its clip, straightened the bandage on his head and flicked a fat, oily grain of soot from his shirt with his right index finger.

Bohlin too climbed up on the roof and looked around.

"For Christ's sake why didn't you shoot?" he said. "I don't get it——"

"No one expects you to," Gunvald Larsson interrupted him. "By the way, have you got a license for that pistol?"

Bohlin shook his head.

"In that case you're probably in trouble," said Gunvald Larsson. "Now come on, let's carry him down."

PER WAHLÖÖ and MAJ SJÖWALL, his wife and co-author, wrote ten Martin Beck mysteries. Mr. Wahlöö, who died in 1975, was a reporter for several Swedish newspapers and magazines and wrote numerous radio and television plays, film scripts, short stories and novels. Maj Sjöwall is also a poet.